# TROLL HUNTERS

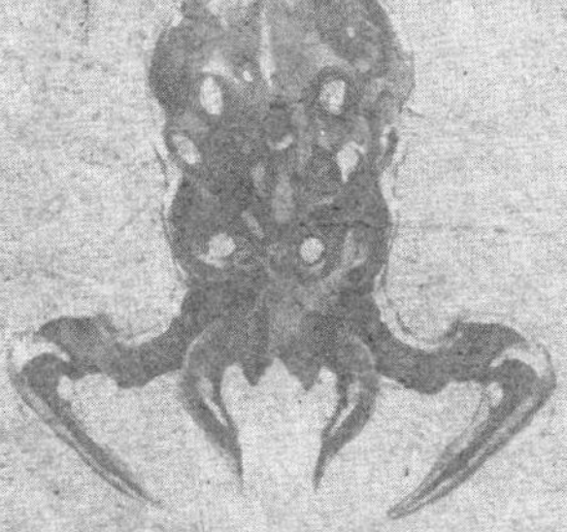

WRITTEN BY MICHAEL DAHL

ILLUSTRATED BY BEN KOVAR

capstone

TROLL HUNTERS is published by Stone Arch Books
A Capstone Imprint
1710 Roe Crest Dr.
North Mankato, Minnesota 56003
www.capstonepub.com

Summary: Far above the small town of Zion Falls, the stars fall from the sky.
Deep below the sleepy city, an ancient evil awakens. Caught in the middle
are four teens with hidden powers beyond their wildest dreams.

Designed by Hilary Wacholz

Cataloging-in-Publication Data is available at the Library of Congress website.
ISBN: 978-1-4342-4590-8

This book is also available in four library-bound editions:
Skyfall                        978-1-4342-3307-3
Dark Tower Rising              978-1-4342-3308-0
The Lava Crown                 978-1-4342-3309-7
Fallen Star                    978-1-4342-3310-3


Printed in China
042012
006680

# TO H.P. LOVECRAFT,
## SPELEOLOGIST

# TABLE OF CONTENTS

# THE FIRST NIGHT

Beneath the roots of tree and vine,
Beneath the grimmest grave,
Beneath the deepest, darkest mine,
Beneath the dimmest cave,

Beneath the vast volcanic lakes,
Beneath the fiery core,
An ancient, ageless Evil wakes
And starts to rise once more.

— from "The Pit of Trolls" by Orson Drood

# 1

County Road One ran east out of Zion Falls, snaked around the north edge of the old, abandoned quarry, and then stretched east again in a straight line. It ran past empty fields, pathless woods, and a few old, weather-beaten houses. Some homes still had people living inside them. A mile from the quarry stood the shack where Lionel Tooker lived with his little girl, Louise.

Lionel Tooker had a red beard, long hair, several hunting rifles, and no patience for other people. Seven-year-old Louise was the same way. Louise preferred to spend time with her rabbits, rather than with her schoolmates. But one morning, Mr. Tooker and his daughter awoke to find that the top half of the wire screen on the rabbit cage in the back yard had been ripped off. Several of the rabbits were missing.

Their back yard bordered on a dark, thick section of woods. Mr. Tooker set up a metal leg hold trap in the woods not far from the rabbit cage.

"Don't worry, Louise," he told the sobbing girl. "We'll catch that big bad wolf. He won't take any more of your bunnies, okay?"

Mr. Tooker didn't really believe it was a wolf that had snatched the furry pets. He was sure it was something smaller, like a coyote or a fox. Mr. Tooker was also sure that the trap would take care of it.

That night, the night the stars fell, Mr. Tooker grabbed a rifle and a flashlight. He wanted to see if his trap had caught anything.

"Stay right there, Louise," he warned. Then he headed into the woods. The little girl, wearing just her nightgown, stood next to the rabbit cage. She held one of her remaining pets in her arms. Its soft ears tickled her chin.

Tooker stepped deeper into the shadow of the

trees. After a few more steps, he disappeared into the darkness. A moment later, he let out a shout.

"It's gone!" Mr. Tooker yelled. The trap had been chained to the thick trunk of an elm tree. But now, the chain, the trap, and half the tree's branches were missing.

"I don't get it," Mr. Tooker said. "What could have done this?"

Something heavy crashed through the bushes behind him.

Mr. Tooker turned around and screamed. Louise dropped her rabbit. It scooted away through the grass and into the darkness. The little girl opened her mouth to yell, but nothing came out. She ran back to the shack and crawled under her bed.

"The big bad wolf," Louise said. "The big bad wolf."

## 2

Less than a mile away from the Tookers' shack, an argument was heating up in the backyard of the O'Ryan home.

"We're not going anywhere tonight," Mr. O'Ryan told his fourteen-year-old son.

"But we have to go see the Draconids," Pablo said. "It's the biggest meteor storm of the century!"

"Draconids?" asked his father. "What are Draconids?"

"The meteors," Pablo explained. "They come from the direction of the constellation Draco.

"We can see them just fine from the backyard," argued his father.

"But the quarry is the best place to watch the shower," said Pablo.

"Why?" his father asked. "The sky looks exactly the same from here."

Pablo's mother was unfolding a plastic lawn chair. "There's that big lake at the bottom of the quarry," she said. "You could see the meteors from above and from below at the same time."

"Like a giant mirror," Pablo added, nodding.

Pablo gazed up at the starry sky. His friends Thora and Bryce were going to the quarry, but he knew that wouldn't make any difference to his father. Mr. O'Ryan was a stubborn man. He was also shy, and he hated crowds. "The sky is big enough to see from right here," Pablo's dad said quietly.

Pablo stormed into the house and then up the stairs to his bedroom. A few moments later, his mother appeared outside his door.

"I just don't understand," said Pablo. "Why can't we go to the quarry?"

"I've already set up the lawn chairs," Mrs. O'Ryan said. "And I brought out the binoculars for you."

"I'm not going to watch," said Pablo. He kicked off his shoes and sat down on his bed.

His mother sighed. "I'd hate for you to miss it," she said. She started to leave, but then turned back to face Pablo. "We'll be outside if you change your mind."

Pablo waited until he heard his mother go through the kitchen and out the back door. Then he locked his door. He had promised Thora that he would meet her and Bryce at the quarry. He was going to keep his word.

He walked to his open window, slipped onto the sill, and eased his way down to the ledge beneath. Then Pablo stretched out his legs, released his grip, and landed on the soft grass in his bare feet. He stood still, listening. His parents were talking in the back yard. Pablo silently headed down the long, winding driveway. A moment later, he was walking along County Road One. The asphalt felt warm on the soles of his feet as he headed west.

The road was dark. There were no streetlights that far out from town. Pablo pressed the light on his watch to check the time. He still had a few minutes before the first meteors would slice through the atmosphere.

Pablo glanced at the deep, grassy ditches that ran along both sides of the road. Beyond the ditches were endless walls of trees, black against the starry sky.

*I must be close to the abandoned Nye farm,* he thought.

The creepy old Nye twins had that deep well on their land. The well that grown-ups had always warned Pablo and his friends about when they were kids. "If you fall in," Pablo's dad had said, "no one will ever find you."

Pablo's thoughts were interrupted by a car rumbling up from behind. He turned just in time to be blinded by a pair of headlights. Pablo quickly stepped aside as a huge SUV whooshed past. *They didn't even slow down,* he thought.

The car was heading west toward the quarry. Pablo recognized the SUV. It belonged to the Fishers. Zak Fisher was in the same grade as Pablo, but they didn't hang out with the same people. Zak was a jock, muscular and talkative. Pablo was the quiet type. He did his homework, kept his head down, and tried his hardest to avoid the school bullies.

Suddenly, the scream of braking tires split the night air. The SUV stopped abruptly, as if it had collided with an invisible wall. The rear window shattered as the hood of the car flew upward. Pablo heard a long, low growl accompanying the cries of human voices. It made him think of a large animal in pain.

Then, just beyond the wreck, Pablo saw what looked like two eyes blink shut. *Did I just imagine that?* he wondered.

Pablo found himself running toward the car. He saw three or four figures inside. One of the passenger doors opened and Zak Fisher staggered out. Blood ran from his nose and forehead.

"O'Ryan," he said. "What are you doing here?"

"Are you all right?" asked Pablo. Zak looked at Pablo blankly for a moment. Then he bent over and threw up in the middle of the road.

Zak stood up, patting his jeans. "I — I have a

phone," he mumbled. As he pulled the cell phone out of his pocket, the crushed device broke into several pieces. "Oh, no . . ."

Pablo thought angrily about his father again. *If my dad would have let me have a cell phone*, he thought, *then I could call 911 right now.*

"Forget it," said Pablo. "I'll run home and get help."

"I'll come with you," said Zak.

"You should stay with your family," said Pablo. But Zak just ran past Pablo, heading down the road. Pablo ran after him.

In minutes, both boys were running up the dirt driveway to the O'Ryan house. Pablo couldn't shake the feeling that something was very wrong. The Fishers' SUV had been totaled, but there was no sign of what it had hit.

*Whatever it was*, Pablo thought, *it must have been big.*

# 3

Thora Gamble stared at the dark, calm lake water while her older brother, Bryce, stared up at the stars. "Hey, did you see that one?" cried Bryce. He shook Thora's shoulder and pointed skyward.

"Yes," she replied. "I see it."

Her brother held his phone at arm's length and snapped a photo. "That's too cool."

In the few minutes since the Draconid shower began, Thora had already seen dozens of the shooting stars. Thora preferred watching the meteors in the giant reflecting pool of the quarry's lake. Seeing the stars far below her feet and overhead at the same time gave her a woozy, floating feeling.

*I feel like I'm flying through the air,* Thora thought, smiling. *Flying like a dragon.*

Staring down at the lake also made Thora feel very alone, as if the crowds of people who surrounded her weren't even there. Just her and the stars above . . .

She barely noticed the oohs and aahs the townspeople breathed whenever an especially bright star skimmed across the sky. For some reason, the arrival of the Draconid shower seemed like a wonderful gift that was just for her. Thora's birthday was only a few days away, so the timing of this spectacular, once-in-a-lifetime event couldn't have been more perfect. Her mind seemed to soar across the stars.

"Oooh, look," Bryce said, snapping Thora back to Earth. "That one's racing right past Orion's belt!"

Thora nodded. She gazed down at the shining meteor that flashed across the watery mirror. Orion was one of the easier constellations to find — Thora could spot Orion's famous belt by the four bright stars in a row.

*Wait — four?* Thora thought, puzzled. *There's only supposed to be three stars.*

Thora blinked and looked again at the starry belt reflected in the quarry's lake. Then Thora counted the stars one more time just to make sure. *Four stars, no doubt about it,* she thought. *Weird.*

Thora quickly glanced back up at the sky. There was the real Orion, blazing overhead, just as he had for centuries, the legendary hunter who had conquered monsters and giant scorpions. Thora gazed at his belt. *One, two, three,* she counted in her head. *Only three stars. That's right.*

But when she looked downward into the lake again, four stars glimmered on Orion's belt.

Thora gasped. The fourth star was moving slowly toward the edge of the lake.

# 4

Pablo was breathing hard as he ran toward his house. But just as he reached the door, he heard his mother scream. When he rushed inside, he saw that Zak had collapsed onto a kitchen chair. More blood stained his hooded sweatshirt.

Pablo's mother grabbed a washcloth from the sink and began gently wiping Zak's face.

"What's wrong?" said Pablo's father, rushing in.

"What happened to you, Zak?" asked Mrs. O'Ryan. Zak didn't respond. He just stared ahead.

"The boy's in shock," said Mr. O'Ryan. He turned toward his son. "Pablo, what is going on?"

Pablo was still gasping from the run. He took a

few deep breaths. "It was an accident," he said. "The Fishers. Their car. Out on the road."

Mr. O'Ryan glared at his son. "What were you doing out on the road?" he asked.

"Zak's parents were hurt in a car accident," Pablo explained to his dad.

Zak suddenly bolted to his feet. "I have to go," he said in a daze. "I have to help them."

"Both you boys should stay right here," said Mrs. O'Ryan.

"I'll go," said her husband. He grabbed a flashlight from a kitchen drawer and pulled his jacket off the hook next to the back door.

"Please, please," said Zak, standing up. "I have to go!"

Mr. O'Ryan braced the boy's shoulders and gently sat him back down. "You're not going anywhere," he said. "Stella, call 911. I'll go see if Zak's parents are all right."

Mr. O'Ryan disappeared out the back door as Pablo's mother snatched at the phone and tapped in the emergency numbers.

Zak touched his nose with the sleeve of his shirt and then looked at it. Blood had dripped onto the fabric. "It's not so bad," Zak said.

"You're missing a shoe," said Pablo.

"Yeah?" Zak looked down. "Well, you're missing both of them." A confused look spread across Zak's dark features. "Were you in the car, too?" he asked.

"You're in shock, Zak," said Pablo.

Zak stared at Pablo. "Please help me."

Pablo felt compelled to look into Zak's eyes. A strange light flickered there. It was something Pablo had never noticed before. It was almost as if a light shone from within them. *Like starlight,* Pablo thought.

It reminded Pablo of the wild eyes he had seen blinking beyond the crushed car hood. Or had he only imagined them in the horrible rush of events?

"Please, Pablo," said Zak. His eyes sparkled.

Pablo nodded.

"Then come on." Zak said. He dashed toward the kitchen door.

Both boys raced outside. "Pablo!" yelled his

mother. But both boys kept running, heading down the driveway to the road.

Pablo's thoughts were racing. *I hope he doesn't pass out while he's running. Is his blood dripping onto the grass? Am I stepping in it? Gross! I'd better watch out for broken glass on the road . . .*

It took them only a few moments to reach the wreck. Smoke rose from the SUV's hood. Mr. O'Ryan was yanking on the driver's door handle. He turned to face the boys as they approached.

"What happened here?" asked Mr. O'Ryan.

"Something ran out onto the road," said Zak, stepping closer. "And that's when —"

The door finally opened with a screech. Pablo's father's eyes went wide.

*Oh, no.* Pablo thought. *Are the Fishers dead?* He raced up beside his father and stared into the car.

It was empty.

# 5

At the lake, Thora scrunched up her nose. "What's that smell?" she asked.

Several children began coughing. The grown-ups standing near the edge of the quarry covered their noses. A few dogs barked and whined.

"Don't look at me," Bryce said, laughing. "She who smelt it, dealt it." But even he was covering his face.

The smell reminded Thora of rotten eggs, old cat litter, and cigarette smoke. She couldn't tell where it was coming from. The lake, maybe? She gazed carefully at the water, but the extra star was gone now.

"I can't take this smell anymore," said Bryce. "Let's go."

Thora and Bryce gathered their things and threw them into his car. Other stargazers were returning to their cars, too. Car engines revved up around the quarry as people waved farewell to their friends and neighbors. But closed doors and windows were no barrier to the overpowering smell.

Bryce and Thora were the only ones headed east. While most of the townsfolk drove west to Zion Falls, the Gambles lived farther east off County Road One.

Thora sniffed. The awful scent was still hanging in the air. "Think it's dangerous?" she asked.

Her brother laughed. "It's probably just sulfur or something like that from the lake," Bryce said. "Whatever it is, it stinks — and it stinks that we had to leave early. Pablo wasn't even there yet."

Thora had once read how people in ancient times sometimes saw glowing gas fumes hovering over swamps. The glow had been mistaken for ghosts. *Maybe the fourth star was just natural gas escaping from the quarry lake,* thought Thora.

"What's that?" asked Bryce.

Thora looked up. Her brother was gripping the

steering wheel so tightly his knuckles were pale. At the far end of the road was an orange glow. A finger of flame flickered behind some trees.

"It's a fire!" said Bryce.

"I hope it's not the O'Ryans' house," said Thora.

"Me too," said Bryce.

Thora's heart pounded. Pablo had promised that he would watch the meteor shower with them at the quarry . . . and Pablo never broke a promise.

"Don't worry," said Bryce. Thora kept gazing at the weird glow. "Maybe it's a forest fire," she said.

Suddenly, a small white figure appeared in the middle of the road. "Look out!" Thora screamed. Bryce shouted and slammed the brake pedal. The car stopped a few feet away from the figure.

"It's a kid," said Bryce.

"It's Louise Tooker!" said Thora. She jumped out of the car and ran over to the little girl.

Louise, still in her nightgown, was screaming and crying. Tears streamed down her face.

"What's wrong?" asked Thora, kneeling down. "Are you okay?"

The little girl ran into Thora's arms and sobbed. "There, there, it's all right," said Thora.

"What's wrong?" asked Bryce. "Is it your house? Is your house on fire?"

The girl continued to sob and gasp. Bryce tapped 911 into his phone.

"What is it, Louise?" asked Thora. Louise gazed up at Thora with fearful eyes.

"Big b-b-bad . . ." she stuttered. Just then, another, larger shape stepped out of the grassy ditch alongside the road. Thora held her breath. It was a man with a red beard, a pale face, and haunted eyes.

"Mr. Tooker!" yelled Bryce.

"That . . . that thing burned down my house," said Lionel Tooker.

Louise buried her head in Thora's shoulder. "The big bad wolf," she cried.

Bryce snapped his phone shut. "They're on their way," he said. "It won't take them long. A fire truck was already headed out this way."

*Another accident?* thought Thora. *What is going on around here?*

Thora glanced up. The meteor shower had grown brighter and more intense. Hundreds of sparkling stars streamed across the sky.

Suddenly, a blood-curdling roar ripped through the darkness. Louise yanked herself free of Thora's arms and ran, screaming, into the ditch alongside the road.

# 6

"Louise! Where are you?" Thora brushed aside the tall grass as she and Bryce ran through the roadside ditch and toward the dark trees.

"Louise!" cried her father. "Come back here!"

The grass became taller as Thora traveled past the line of dark trees and into the woods. She lost sight of the others. Their voices grew muffled and distant. All she heard was the swish of the grass as it brushed against her shoulders.

Thora looked up. Silently, the Draconid meteor shower was still lighting up the evening sky. She pushed through more grass. Her shoes were getting damp. "Louise!" she called.

Then, from the corner of Thora's eye, she saw a small white figure. It dashed ahead of her and vanished behind a tree trunk. "Bryce!" yelled Thora. "I see her. She's here in the woods."

No one answered. Thora awkwardly moved through the dense grass and trees. She grasped at the low tree branches to pull herself through. Within the shadow of the woods, she screamed, "Louise!" Nothing moved over the spongy forest floor. No twigs snapped. No bushes rustled. "Louise!" Thora called again. Nothing.

Thora pushed her way deeper into the woods. The forest grew darker and darker. Now, the roof of branches above her blocked out the starlight. Darkness was draped thickly around her. Thora shivered. "I'm lost," she said to herself.

Then Thora heard a voice. A girl's voice. Singing.

*"Within the wood*
*There lies a house,*
*And in the house, a room,*
*Where Someone sits and waits for me,*
*Hiding in the gloom."*

"Louise?!" cried Thora. "Is that you?"

*"Then Someone soon will whisper*
*And pull me to my doom,*
*Within the wood,*
*Within the house,*
*Within that little room."*

Thora walked nervously toward the voice. She stopped when she saw a large, rounded shape. The object was hard to see against the dark trees beyond. It looked far too large to be a little girl.

*Is that you, Louise?* Thora thought nervously.

"Yes," came a voice from the shadow. "It's me, Thora. I'm hiding in this bush."

*How did she know what I'm thinking?* Thora thought. "But I can't see you," Thora said.

"I'm right here," came the voice. "Come closer."

The black shape shivered, as if a breeze had brushed it. But there was no wind.

"Thora!" someone yelled from behind.

As Thora turned, she saw Pablo standing with Zak Fisher, another boy from school. Pablo held a flashlight, and there was blood on his face.

"What are you doing here, Pablo?!" Thora asked.

Pablo blinked. "We're looking for —"

A roar shook the forest. Thora turned back. The black shape shivered. It jerked and twisted, unfolding itself. Branches became knees and elbows. Twigs turned into hands. Long spindly fingers reached, claw-like, toward the sky.

Thora screamed as Zak's flashlight partially illuminated the growing mass. Lizard-like eyes, black and oily, blinked back at them. The shadow rose higher. It stood tall and thick and jagged like a tree. A giant hand reached toward Thora.

"Get back!" shouted Zak. He aimed his flashlight's beam directly at the creature's eyes. It roared again and covered its face.

Suddenly, bright light grew in the woods, as though a door had been opened in a dark room. Whiteness blazed around them. Thora could see every single leaf on the ground beneath her feet.

"Get back!" Zak shouted at the creature. "Get back, you — you whatever!" He shoved the flashlight closer toward the oily pupils. Thora looked up,

shielding her eyes against the growing brightness. She ignored the monster's roars and stared. A second unbelievable figure was rising in the clearing.

It was a centaur.

# 7

Years ago, Pablo had read a thick book of Greek myths. He distinctly remembered a half-man, half-horse creature called the centaur that was strong and fearsome. In the forest before him now, the centaur was more powerful than he could have ever imagined. The creature's long white hair fell onto his broad shoulders. His four legs ended in gleaming white hooves.

The centaur's muscular arms aimed a gigantic bow at the shadowy monster. In one quick movement, his huge hand pulled back an arrow and released it into the night. The tip of the arrow blazed with the brightness of a shooting star as it dug itself into the

monster's chest. A scream thundered against their ears as the monster ripped the arrow out and threw it down. As the blazing light fell at Pablo's feet, he saw that it was not an arrow. At least not anymore. It was a safety flare, with one end sputtering like a welder's torch. When Pablo looked up, the centaur was gone.

"Over here!" shouted a strange voice. A man was standing behind them, waving his arms at them. "Hurry!" he yelled. "Before its eyes adjust to the light!" He turned and broke into a sprint in the other direction.

Thora, Pablo, and Zak immediately ran after the mysterious man. Soon, they emerged onto the road once again.

They came to a stop by an SUV with its headlights off and its engine running. All of them were out of breath and panting — except for Thora, Pablo noticed. "You don't even look tired!" he said.

Thora smiled at him. "Looks like all that running at track practice finally paid off," she said.

"There's no time for chit-chat!" urged the man, swinging open the door to his SUV. "Quick — get in!"

Pablo held his friends back. "Wait," he said, narrowing his eyes. "How do we know we can trust you?"

"You mean, aside from the fact that I just saved your lives?" the man answered with a smirk.

Pablo hesitated. Although he didn't know the man, he didn't see any other options. "Fine," Pablo said.

As soon as all of them had clambered into the SUV, it shot forward. Thora, Pablo, and Zak were hurled back against their seats. Branches scraped at the SUV's sides.

"Turn on your headlights!" yelled Zak.

"I don't want the others to see us," the man said.

"What others?" asked Thora. She turned and glanced over at Pablo, who was staring out the back window.

"The one back there, once it recovers, can easily find us even without seeing us," said the strange man. "And there's a group of them out tonight. A scouting party. I don't want to attract their attention."

"There are more of them?" asked Zak.

"Yes," the man said gravely. "Many, many more."

The SUV plunged over a deep rut.

"What exactly was that thing?" asked Thora.

"It has many names," said the man. "In its own language, it calls itself *gathool*. But most experts simply call them trolls."

*Trolls?* A lump settled in Pablo's throat.

Zak laughed. "You've got to be kidding! You mean, like in *Lord of the Rings?* That's fairy tales."

The strange man gave a bitter laugh. "Was it a fairy tale that crashed into your parent's car this evening?" he asked.

Zak's face went white. "How do you know about that?" he asked.

"Hold tight!" said the man. The vehicle bounced over a series of bumps and then stopped suddenly. "I've got to get that driveway fixed," he said, opening the door. "Well, we're here. Quick, into the house."

"What about Louise?" said Thora, her voice beginning to shake. "And I have to find my brother!"

"We will," said the man. "But we won't do them any good if we let that troll catch us. Now hurry."

A dark building rose among the trees. In a single window, dim lights glowed. The place reminded Pablo of something. An old nursery rhyme from his childhood about a house in the woods . . .

"You're all in danger," the man warned. "You can't stay out here in the car. Please. You can trust me."

Pablo looked hard at the man's face. He seemed younger than Pablo had first thought. The man had wild hair and high cheekbones. His eyes were hard to see inside the dim SUV. But then Pablo saw something flash in them. Starlight.

"Come on," Pablo said to the other two. Then he whispered to Thora, "I think he's okay." He gave her a small smile. Thora nodded back.

They slipped out of the car and followed their guide through a yard full of weeds, then onto a solid stone porch. Zak kept glancing back over his shoulder, peering warily into the darkness around them.

# 8

Pablo shivered. The night was nearly silent. In the sky above, stars still twinkled, but the meteor shower had stopped.

The mysterious man who led them into the building wore a long cape over his shirt and jeans. In the light that poured from a round window in the door, Pablo thought he saw something. In the shadows of the man's cape, he swore he saw a third arm.

Once they were inside, the man led them up a long flight of winding stone stairs, using only a flash-light as a guide. "Isn't it safer downstairs?" asked Zak.

"If those creatures get inside, it won't matter where we are," said the man.

After a few minutes of climbing, Pablo was gasping for breath. "How high do these stairs go?" he asked. "We must have climbed three stories."

"Four," said the man. "Oh, and here we are." The stairs ended. He pushed open an old, heavy oak door and ushered them inside.

"Wow!" whispered Pablo.

The eight-sided room was spacious. Tall windows on four sides faced the points of the compass drawn on the floor. Starlight flooded into the room, revealing tables and scientific equipment. The other four walls were lined with floor-to-ceiling bookcases.

The entire countryside was visible from this height. Pablo could see the edge of the quarry, and the fields beyond the forest. *Weird*, thought Pablo. *I don't remember seeing a tower outside.*

"Ah," said the man. "A full moon." He walked to a window and picked up a pair of binoculars from the windowsill.

Pablo noticed how thick the stone windowsills

were. *The whole place must be built from quarry stones,* he thought.

Thora grabbed his shoulder. "This room," she whispered. "It doesn't make sense. It's bigger than his whole house!"

"I know," Pablo whispered back. "What's going on?"

Zak walked toward the man. He stood face to face with him. "You seem to know a lot about us," he said, "but we don't even know who you are."

"And what were you doing back there in the forest?" asked Pablo.

The man lowered the binoculars and turned to them. "I was there because I knew that's where the trolls would meet to join forces," he said. "According to my research, it's halfway between the two entry points to the surface."

"The quarry," said Thora. "So that weird smell was coming from those monsters?"

"Yes — to both questions," said the man.

"But who are you?" asked Zak.

"Hoo," the man said.

"Yeah, man — who are you?!" said Zak.

"Um, that's me," said the man. "Hoo. Dr. Hoo, actually."

Pablo eyed Dr. Hoo up and down, noticing the strange clothes he wore. "What kind of doctor are you?" Pablo asked.

"I'm a doctor of several things," said Dr. Hoo. "But most recently, cryptozoology."

"What's that?" asked Zak.

Dr. Hoo sat down on a window seat, facing his curious guests. "It's the study of hidden or secret creatures," he answered. "The kinds of creatures whose existence hasn't been scientifically proven."

"Like Bigfoot?" asked Thora.

"Or the Loch Ness monster?" added Pablo.

"How about trolls?" added Zak, with a grin.

"Or the yeti, the chupacabra, unicorns, the orange pendek, the giant squid — which, by the way, has been proven to exist," the doctor added.

"And centaurs?" said Pablo, staring at the doctor.

"Exactly. Like centaurs," Dr. Hoo said. "Half human, half beast." He stood up quickly, his cape wrapped carefully around him, and pointed out the window. "Did you know that the centaur is the only creature to have two constellations named after it?"

Zak crossed his arms. "So, what's the deal with those other creatures?" he asked. "The trolls."

"And how do you know so much about them?" asked Thora.

The doctor raced over to a wooden table covered with books, papers, and maps. Dr. Hoo pointed at a pile of books at one end. "These books were recently brought to me by a colleague," he said. "She and I met online while we were both studying the *gathool*. Her great-uncle, in fact, was the first person to discover their existence. And these are his books."

Pablo walked closer and read some of the weird titles. *The Pit of Trolls. The Call of Cthulhu. Servants of the Graveyard.*

"I have been hunting through these tomes to find the creatures' weaknesses," said the doctor. "I mean, everyone knows that trolls can be destroyed by fire or acid in stories and video games. But that's not real life."

The house trembled. Books spilled off the table. In the distance, there was a roar.

"Well, I sure hope you found it, Doc," said Zak.

The room shook again. This time, books fell from several of the tall bookcases. Suddenly, Zak screamed. The doctor swung his flashlight around toward Zak. An insect-like creature the size of a large cat had its thick claws wrapped around Zak's head. "Get it off me!" he yelled. "Get it off!"

"Relax," said the doctor. "It's only a coconut crab. And it's stuffed."

Zak threw the lifeless hulk to the floor. "Why was it hanging from the ceiling?" he shouted.

"That's the only place I had room for it," said the doctor.

A louder roar came from outside.

"It's getting closer!" said Thora.

The doctor dug through the clutter on the table. He handed each of them a small orange pistol.

"Flare guns," Dr. Hoo explained. "In case of emergency. Aim directly at the creature's eyes and pull the trigger. It will blind them long enough for you to run away." Then he handed out small red cartridges. "These are the flares. Keep them on you."

Pablo stuffed a couple of flares in his pockets. He held one of the flares up in front of his face. "Could one of these start a forest fire?" he asked.

"Who cares? It's better than getting caught by one of those things," said Zak. "Hey, maybe a fire isn't such a bad idea! Doc, do trolls burn?"

"The *gathool* can survive temperatures up to 1200 degrees Celsius," said the doctor. "Some of them live next to magma streams deep within the earth."

"So I guess fire's out," said Zak.

The room shook. A spiderweb of cracks appeared in several of the windows.

"Where are they?" asked Thora.

The door opened. A ghostly shape appeared at the top of the dark staircase. The doctor aimed his flashlight beam at it. Standing there, blinking in the light, was a small girl in a white nightgown.

9

"Louise!" said Thora. Louise ran to her.

"I heard it again," said the little girl. "It's getting closer."

"How did you get here?" Thora asked.

"The doctor brought me," said Louise.

"Oh, she's the girl you were looking for?" Dr. Hoo said. "I found her wandering outside earlier."

"Dr. Hoo, did you find the creatures' weakness?" Pablo asked. "Is there a way to stop them?"

Dr. Hoo picked up one of the books from the pile on the table. "Yes, I'm afraid there is," he said.

"Afraid?" repeated Thora.

"You're not going to like it," said the doctor,

flipping through the pages. "At least not right now, because it can't help us. Sunlight is the one thing that can destroy the *gathool*."

"There's at least seven hours until dawn," said Zak.

Thora shook her head. She felt weird talking about this. How could any of it be true? But she had seen the monster with her own eyes. Everyone else in the room had seen it too. And she had heard it singing to her in the forest. In Louise's voice. Trying to lure her closer. To trap her.

"Listen, I know those things out there are real," said Thora. "But are you sure about sunlight? I mean, that really does sound like a fairy tale. The sun comes up and turns a troll into stone?"

"It has something to do with their chemical makeup," said the doctor. "Their bodies can't process the sun's radiation, which is probably what drove them to live underground in the first place." He tossed the book aside and grabbed another. "And they don't exactly turn to stone. It's more like meteoric rock. It's in their DNA. Some scientists think that's how the trolls got to earth in the first place. On rocks from outer space. Meteors, maybe."

Dr. Hoo furiously flipped through the pages of the book. "Folklore usually does contain at least a small element of truth," he pointed out. "Ah, here it is."

He read aloud. "An ancient prophecy among the *gathool* has warned them for centuries of a deadly 'band of light' that could destroy their species. But the *gathool* vocabulary is small; their mouths are limited in the sounds they can make. So few words must stand for many things. 'Band' can also mean 'ring,' 'circle,' or 'sphere.' 'Light' can also stand for 'gold,' 'shining,' or 'pain.' Most experts believe the old tradition of sunlight being harmful to trolls is true. And since the two most powerful rings of light are obviously the sun and —"

The doctor stopped. "There's something outside," he whispered. He quietly walked over to a window.

The others followed him. Louise began to whimper. Thora put her arm around the little girl.

"What's over there?" asked Pablo, pointing past the field.

"That field is straight east of this house," said the doctor. "It runs parallel to County Road One."

"That's back toward the Tooker house," Pablo said. "And the accident where everything started."

"Precisely," said Doctor Hoo. "You see, according to the old survey maps of Zion Falls, there's a deep well over there. It's likely the trolls used it as an entry point to the surface, as well as the tunnels in the old quarry."

"I know that well!" said Pablo. "It's on the land next to ours. We were always told to stay far away from it."

"Why did they need an entry point?" asked Zak. "I mean, what do they want? Why are they here?"

"They want to take back the surface world," said the doctor. "Thousands of years ago, their kind dominated humans. They raised us like livestock."

"Like cows?" asked Pablo.

"More like hamburger," Dr. Hoo said. "Those creatures out there are hungry. They have traveled from far underground and they need food. Us."

"Something's moving out there!" said Thora. She

pointed toward the line of trees at the edge of the field. Tall shadows swayed beneath the motionless branches.

Pablo looked out at the field and the trees and the sky. He saw something that reminded him of science class. They had been studying astronomy, which is one reason he and Thora and Bryce were watching the meteor shower that night. Their teacher had been talking about the planet Earth and how it was a part of a larger solar system. Solar. The ring of light.

"That's it — the moon!" Pablo blurted out. "That's how we can defeat the trolls. Not in seven hours, but right now!"

Everyone stared confusedly at Pablo. Just as Pablo was about to explain, the house shook more fiercely than before. Windows broke. Shelves toppled. Something made a loud crash at the bottom of the staircase.

"I have to slow them down," said the doctor, moving away from the window.

"Where are you going?" asked Zak.

As the doctor stopped at the door, his cape swirled

around him like a robe. Once more, Pablo was sure he saw a third arm held closely to the doctor's side. "No matter what happens," Dr. Hoo commanded. "Do not open this door."

"But, Doctor, I figured it out," said Pablo. "We can use the moon to —"

"I repeat, stay right here," said Dr. Hoo. "And do not open this door under any circumstances!" He gave Pablo a quick, knowing look, and then shut the door behind him. They heard a sharp metallic click as the door sealed shut.

"Did he just lock us in?" said Zak. "I think he just locked us in."

A steady bluish-white light poured out from the keyhole and the space beneath the door. It blazed brighter and brighter, as if a searchlight were on the other side.

Another crashing sound rose up from below. Louise started to cry. Thora grabbed her and ran to the center of the room.

"Thora," said Pablo, "remember what Mr. Thomas was talking about in science class last month?"

Thora was busily checking her flare gun to see if it was loaded. "What?" she said.

"The moon!" Pablo repeated. "It doesn't produce its own light. The moon only glows because of —"

"Reflected sunlight!" Thora exclaimed, remembering. "Do you think it will work?"

"If the fairy tales are real," Pablo said.

# 10

"First, we have to get them away from the trees," said Pablo.

"What are you two talking about?" asked Zak.

The octagonal room stopped shaking. The crashing sounds from below also stopped.

"The moon," said Thora. "The full moon is coming up."

"Yeah, so?" said Zak.

"So, that's sunlight," said Pablo. "Sunlight kills trolls. Or turns them into meteoric rock," Thora said. "Or whatever."

Zak stared at the yellow moon that was rising above the tops of the distant trees. "That's brilliant!"

he said. "Better than anything the doc came up with, anyway."

*That's not true,* Thora thought. *Dr. Hoo did mention there was a full moon. But —*

Thora's thoughts were interrupted by a knock at the door. Everyone froze.

"Let me in," said a familiar voice.

"Dr. Hoo, is that you?" asked Pablo.

"Of course it is," came the reply. "Don't worry, the trolls are gone now. I was able to scare them away for good."

"Finally, some good news," said Zak. He stepped toward the door.

"No!" Thora yelled at Zak. Then she lowered her voice to a whisper. "It's a trick."

"Thora, just let me in," repeated the voice. "Now."

"But you told us not to open it," she answered.

They heard the doctor chuckle. "So I did," the voice said. "But it's all over now. The creatures have moved outside."

Thora shook her head. "The real doctor would use his key," she whispered. She remembered the troll back in the forest clearing and how it had sung to her — it had spoken using Louise's voice.

"Did you find Louise out there?" Thora asked.

"But she's right —" Zak began.

Thora grabbed his arm and squeezed it. Then she turned to look at Louise and put her finger to her lips.

"Did you, Doctor?" Thora repeated. "Did you find Louise?"

There was a pause.

Then the doctor chuckled softly. "Yes, Thora, I did," he said. "She's standing right here with me."

"Let me in," came a little girl's voice. "I'm scared."

Louise began to shake. She clutched Thora's leg with both her arms.

"I don't like it out here," came the false voice again. "Please let me inside, Thora. Please, open the door."

Zak aimed his flare gun at the door. "Now what do we do?" he whispered.

"It's coming," said the fake girl's voice, this time more loudly. "Thora, it's coming closer. Don't let it get us! Let me in!"

The real Louise pulled away from Thora. She ran to the door and pounded on it. "Get away from us, you monster!" Louise screamed.

A tremendous roar rattled the door on its frame. Then a deep, angry voice roared out. "You will be my dinner, you little brats!"

# 11

Louise screamed and ran back to Thora.

Zak walked over to a broken window and looked down. "So we need to get those monsters out in the field under the moon," he said. "If I can get down from up here, I could run out there and make them follow me."

"We'll need some rope," agreed Pablo.

Thora, Zak, and Pablo raced through the room, searching through shelves and drawers and piles of cardboard boxes. All of them were rifling through the room, desperate to find something useful.

"Up there!" Louise cried out. Coils and coils of rope hung from hooks, attached to the ceiling.

The boys yanked down all of the rope and tied two lengths of it together. Then they threw the free ends out the east and the south windows. Pablo and Zak climbed up on the sills, preparing to rappel down the smooth rock walls.

"I can run too, you know," said Thora.

"Someone has to watch the kid," said Zak, pointing at Louise. He looked out the window, but just as he was starting to lean out, he collapsed to the floor. Pablo and Thora ran to him.

"I . . . I can't stand," Zak said.

Pablo pulled him into a chair. "It must be the shock," said Pablo. "It finally caught up to you."

"What do you mean?" asked Thora.

"Zack was in a car accident earlier this evening," Pablo explained. "And his parents vanished."

"Are you going to be all right, Zak?" Thora said worriedly.

Zak bent over, his face in his hands. "This can't be happening to me," he muttered.

"Zak can't make the sprint to the field," Pablo explained.

Thora bent down and whispered to Louise, "You have to look after him for us, okay?"

The little girl nodded. "I want a flare gun," she whispered back. Thora smiled.

Zak groaned into his hands. "Watch him," Thora repeated to Louise.

Thora and Pablo returned to the windows, gripped the ropes, and swung their legs over the ledge.

"Be careful," Louise whispered.

"You too," said Pablo.

They began to descend. Below them, the house's windows blazed with bluish-white light. Quickly, the two climbers shimmied down the ropes.

Dr. Hoo had said the library room was five stories above the ground. It felt much higher to Pablo. The outside walls of the octagonal tower were made of smooth stone blocks. Because their windows faced different directions, Pablo and Thora couldn't always see one another as they descended to the ground. But Pablo heard Thora grunting and breathing hard just like he was.

Then, just as Pablo was lowering himself past

a window, the light from within disappeared. The window's glass was gone, and curtains fluttered toward him.

A heavy hand as large as a tree trunk reached out through the window. Its seven fingers opened and shut like a metal trap.

Pablo pushed himself away from the smooth wall. He swung away from the hand, his body spinning on the rope. As he neared a window on the other side, its glass shattered. Another hand, as large as the first, twisted outward, hunting for prey.

Pablo's momentum propelled him directly toward the hand. He loosened his grip on the rope so he'd slide down faster. Ten feet beneath the grasping claws, he tightened his grasp. The rope burned like fire as he came to a stop.

Pablo looked up at the angry hand above him as it clawed through the air. It pulled itself back inside the window. Then, just as Thora dropped down, the hand shot out again. Its rough fingers grabbed her legs.

"Thora!" Pablo yelled. "Help!"

Pablo tried to climb back up, but his palms were

bloody from their slide down the rope. It felt as if a knife had sliced into his hands.

"Move, Thora!" he shouted.

Thora kicked at the huge hand as it pulled her toward the window. A creature hissed from inside the house. Then, a deep blackness yawned open from within the window. The troll was opening its mouth!

Pablo suddenly remembered his flare gun. He tugged it from his belt. But just as he was about to fire, he heard a fizzing sound come from above him.

A flare hit the troll's hand and exploded. Its blaze lit up the darkness like a tiny white sun. The stinking breath of the monster struck Pablo's face as its scream burst through the window. The hand writhed in pain and released the Thora's legs.

The two climbers looked up. A small white face was staring down at them from the library window. Louise waved at them, a flare gun in her other hand.

Then Zak's face appeared. "I tried to stop her," he shouted.

Pablo hurried down the rope. The pain in his hands was almost unbearable, so he had to pinch his feet together to support his body's weight. Slowly, he lowered himself like an inchworm toward the ground until his bare feet hung only a few yards from the earth.

Suddenly, a huge crash shook the entire house. A troll burst through the wall and onto the ground.

"Run!" Zak shouted from the window.

# 12

Pablo fell to the grass in a crouch. Thora landed a few feet away. They both leaped up and raced away from the doctor's tower.

Up in the library, Zak grabbed the flare pistol from Louise, reloaded it, and shot. A flare rocketed toward the troll and exploded on the ground in front of it. The sudden light stunned the creature. It covered its eyes and fell to its side as Pablo and Thora ran toward the field.

*Thanks for the head start, Zak,* thought Thora.

But in moments, Thora heard the monster roaring furiously behind them again. Then she heard the same noise coming from her right.

*The creature's companions!* Thora realized. *They're all chasing us now!*

Without saying a word, Thora pointed toward the wall of trees that separated them from the field. Pablo nodded. They both swung off to their left, and the trolls followed them.

Two of the monsters were larger than the rest. Because of their size, they needed fewer strides to cover more ground. Their enormous feet thudded closer and closer to Thora and Pablo. And behind them came the third troll from the house. All of them were gaining speed, and all of them were hungry. If Thora and Pablo didn't pick up speed, the trolls would soon overtake them.

Thora gritted her teeth and sucked in the air. She forced herself not to look back at the trolls. Instead, she concentrated on her breathing. She thought about track practice at school, and listened to the thumping of her feet against the soft forest ground. She thought of her brother Bryce, who always watched her race from the sidelines and cheered for her. She breathed deeper. Her lungs pulled in more and more air.

Then she noticed two especially large trees up ahead. The tall elms were directly in front of her. They stood only a few feet apart, and beyond them was the open field. Thora blocked out every sound, every sight, every thought. She didn't even remember that Pablo was running right behind her.

All she thought about was those trees. They were the finish line. Her goal. She ran faster and faster, pushing all of her strength into her legs and her pumping arms. Her breath and the thudding of her feet joined in a single rhythm.

*Watch me, Bryce,* she thought. *Watch me win.*

At the tree line, the first troll reached out a spiky arm. Thora ducked her head just as a stony claw smashed right through a thick-trunked tree. The impact was so close that Thora felt the splinters brush against her cheeks. But she just pumped her legs even harder.

Then she was in the field. "Keep running, Thora!" Pablo was the one screaming behind her, but Thora's ears heard Bryce, urging her onward.

Thora stared across the field. The moon was

rising. She saw moonlight shining on a wire fence at the far end. That fence became her finish line.

Her shoes thudded against the packed dirt of the field. Waist-high grass, hollow as straws, brushed against her calves. The thudding of her feet grew louder. The ground trembled with each step. It was the trolls — they were still following her. Their massive legs pounded like tree trunks smashing into the earth.

She didn't dare turn to look. A backward glance would slow her down. Thora's track coach had always told her to keep staring straight ahead when she ran. Set a goal, run toward it. That's all she had to do. Just one thing in the world. Breathe and run. Breathe and run. A few hundred times. That's all. Thora heard another yell behind her. She recognized Pablo's voice this time, but she didn't understand what he was saying. She kept her focus on the wire fence shining in the moonlight.

The fence seemed to glitter. Thora took in deeper breaths. She lowered her head and happened to glance at her feet.

*Why are my shoes all white?* Thora thought. *I know I put on dark ones this morning.*

The ground looked different, too. The field was white with light. The light was so intense, it was like she was running on snow. Then the light grew brighter. All color and shadow drained away. Whiteness engulfed her like a blizzard. *Am I about to pass out?* Thora thought. *Or my eyes are playing tricks on me. Maybe I'm not getting enough oxygen.*

Her feet thudded with each step. Her heart beat even faster. Her eyes were almost blinded by the light. A hand brushed against her hair, trailing behind her like a dark flag. She stifled a scream, and pumped her arms harder. She brushed sweat out of her eyes. She looked at the field below her. Every blade of grass, every clump of dirt shimmered in the moonlight. Or reflected sunlight, as Pablo had said.

The heavy pounding behind her had stopped. But Thora didn't turn back. She kept racing toward the wire fence.

"Thora!" Pablo yelled. He was in trouble. Thora had to help him.

She slowed and quickly looked behind her. She didn't see Pablo or the trolls. Just three massive mounds of smoldering rock rested in the middle of the field. How had she missed them?

Thora bent over, resting her hands on her knees. The she heard a rough, scrambling sound. She looked up. Someone appeared from behind the rocky mound nearest her. It was Pablo, and he was grinning.

"You did it!" Pablo shouted, pointing at the rocks.

"Huh?" Thora said. She stared hard at the mounds of rock. They resembled grotesque bodies. Chunks that looked like legs and arms and shoulders rested at the sides. And all three had twisted, monstrous heads.

Thora couldn't speak. She could only stare, wide-eyed, at the petrified trolls.

"You led them into the moonlight, and they turned to stone!" said Pablo. "It worked! It really worked!"

Thora fell in a heap on the ground, smiling. Her legs felt like they were on fire. Her eyes burned from her own salty sweat. Her chest heaved with each breath, but she didn't care. She was too happy to care.

# 13

Pablo sat in the field next to Thora, quietly waiting for her to catch her breath after their desperate race with the trolls. He gazed up at the sky. The full moon sailed serenely overhead, oblivious to the fact that it had saved their lives. The meteor shower was over, but for some reason, the stars seemed to glow with an added brilliance.

"We just lived through a fairy tale," Pablo finally said.

Thora nodded. "But this isn't the happy ending," she said.

"No, not yet," Pablo said. He knew they still had to find Bryce, and Zak's parents, and take Louise back to her father. They had to find out what had happened to Doctor Hoo, too. And Pablo still had questions about the centaur he had seen back in the clearing, and about the third arm he had glimpsed beneath the doctor's cape. Not to mention the strange light that had seemed to extend outward from Thora as she ran through the field.

But all that could wait. Right now, here in this moment, Pablo felt hopeful.

Something had changed that night for all of them. For him and Thora and Zak. And even for little Louise.

And somehow, Pablo knew that it was just the beginning.

# THE SECOND NIGHT

Darkness beats his Dreadful Drums —
The Shadow comes! The Shadow comes!
Darkness cries to every Ear —
The Palaces of Night are here!
Behold the Chambers deep and dim,
Behold the Towers gaunt and grim,
Behold the Throne that carries him,
Behold the Shadow comes!

— from "Servants of the Graveyard"
   by Anthony Atwood Crake

# 14

Pablo awoke with a start. He found himself reclined in a wide, grassy field. The pale October sun was just beginning to rise over the treetops. It cast a beautiful glow upon the field. Slowly, he realized he was still in the field with the petrified trolls.

*Where's Thora?!* Pablo thought in a panic. He swiveled his head around to find that Thora was sleeping soundly right next to him. *We must have fallen asleep,* Pablo thought.

*Hroom . . . hroom . . .*

A strange noise made Pablo shiver. He turned his head. His gaze met a pair of dark, unblinking eyes. They bulged from mushroom-colored skin, and were as dark as a bottomless pit. Pablo squinted against the morning light. Now he could see that the dark eyes sat atop a wart-covered body about the size of a football. It collapsed, then swelled up again.

Pablo chuckled. *Just a toad,* he thought. *A big one.*

Pablo pinched his eyes shut. When he opened them, he saw that there were at least a dozen of the amphibians sitting and warming themselves on the petrified remains of a troll. Mist rose from the grotesque statue's jagged, rocky sides. A second troll statue, behind the first, was also covered with the cold-blooded creatures.

*Hroom . . . hroom . . .*

The toads were croaking deep within their throats. It sounded like the beating of faraway drums. Just a few hours ago, those statues had been living creatures, chasing him and Thora, hungry for human blood. Their blood.

"Pablo, are you okay?" asked Thora's sleepy voice. She slowly sat up, watching Pablo with drowsy eyes.

"Yeah, I'm fine," he said, pointing at the croaking creature. "Hey, look at all these frogs."

Thora glanced toward Pablo's finger. "Eww, they're everywhere!" she said. After a moment's pause, she added, "They sure seem to like the petrified trolls."

Pablo nodded. "Feel how warm the statues are," he said.

They both held out their hands as if warming themselves by a campfire. The statues' jagged, limb-like edges gave them a frightful appearance.

"The doctor was right," Thora said. "The trolls look just like meteors when they're petrified."

Pablo glanced at the rocky shapes. "Technically, they'd be meteorites," he said. "That's what you call a meteoroid that lands on earth. A meteor is the flash of light we see when it streaks through the sky. That's what we saw last night during the meteor shower."

"Did you learn that in Mr. Thomas's science class?" Thora asked.

"I think I read it in one of my dad's science magazines," said Pablo. "Pretty geeky, huh?"

Thora shrugged. "Not really," she lied, standing up stiffly. She gazed around the empty field. "I need to find my brother."

Pablo turned to Thora. "Where did you last see Bryce?" he asked.

"We were all looking for Louise in the woods," Thora replied. "Bryce, Louise's father, and I got separated before Dr. Hoo saved us."

"I didn't see Bryce when Zak and I found you," said Pablo.

"Bryce left his car in the middle of the road," said Thora. "That's when we all started searching for Louise. But I know he wouldn't leave me behind. Bryce has to be around here somewhere."

Pablo considered the awful size and speed of the trolls. A lone teenager wouldn't stand a chance against even one of them. Then again, Pablo and the others had somehow managed to survive the night. Perhaps Bryce had, too.

*Hroooooooom . . . hrooom . . .*

One of the toads sitting on the rock opened its big mouth and yawned. It had teeth — a double row of sharp fangs that glistened with drool.

Pablo was confused. *Toads don't have teeth like that,* he thought. *What in the world are these things?*

The constant croaking started to make Pablo feel uneasy. "Uh, let's go back to the house," he said, standing up. "We should check on Zak and Louise."

"Do you think they're —" Thora began.

The sound of a strong gust of wind interrupted her. But there were no leaves moving on the nearby branches, and Pablo felt no breeze against his skin.

Thora pointed at some tall grass. "Look!" she cried.

The trees were not moving, but the grass was. It swayed in a great wave, as if an invisible hand was sweeping across the field. Pablo squinted his eyes and realized the grass was being pushed aside by something closer to the ground. And it was coming straight toward them.

"What's going on?" Pablo said, taking a step back.

Just then, countless snakes slid out from the grass. Their slithering shapes created a great river of brown and black and gray. They slid over and under each other, sunlight glistening off their scales.

"There must be thousands of them!" Thora exclaimed. "We have to get out of here!'

"Wait!" said Pablo. "They aren't attacking us."

Every snake moved straight ahead, traveling toward a distant point on the horizon. "It looks like they're heading for the Nye farm," Thora said. "To the well."

Pablo stuck out a bare foot and placed it in the path of the serpents. They slid around his ankle as if it were a small tree in the path of a flood. Thora hesitated briefly, then joined him. Slowly, they made their way through the serpentine river.

"Let's go find Dr. Hoo," Pablo said. "I bet he'll know what's up with all these snakes."

Thora nodded. "And he'll know how to find my brother."

# 15

A small white rental car drove through Zion Falls just before sunrise. It passed the abandoned quarry, where a heavy cloud of mist loomed over the lake. It continued past several abandoned farms and empty fields. Then it traveled past a long stretch of dark trees and into a lonely field.

It pulled onto the gravel-covered shoulder, and then stopped. Mara Lovecraft stepped out of the car. The young woman wore dark jeans, boots, and a long gray coat. Her straight black hair was tied back in a long ponytail. She found her smart phone and checked a digital map of the area. The local homes and farms were all highlighted.

"Gamble, Tooker, O'Ryan . . . and Nye," she read.

She tapped the screen on the Nye farm and zoomed in. Then she lifted her head and stared at the far side of the field toward an old house, a few farm buildings, and a rusty silo.

"There it is," she said.

Mara looked up at the dark, early morning sky and frowned. She was sorry that she had missed the meteor shower the night before. Mara heard it had been spectacular, but she had been too busy driving all night to see it. Her friend and colleague Dr. Hoo had assured her that Zion Falls would soon be the site of an even greater natural event. Dr. Hoo said that Mara's help would be needed soon. That the future of the entire world depended on it.

Mara remote-locked the car, then stepped into the tall, wet grass. After a few minutes of walking, she had crossed only half of the field.

A shiver shot through her. Mara turned up her coat collar against the cold air and continued walking. *What has Dr. Hoo gotten me into this time?* she wondered.

The ground beneath Mara's feet shuddered. She bent her head to listen. A loud moan came from directly beneath her feet. Mara smiled. She muttered a few words in a strange language toward the earth.

A moan called back to answer her. But it was not just a moan. There were words. Mara spoke again. Suddenly, the field shook fiercely as the ground rose up in front of her.

The earth moved in rippling waves. Soil, rocks, leaves, and grass heaved upward into the shape of a wall. The wall turned and twisted, its sides sloping down. Weird shapes jutted out. Shapes like legs and arms.

A breeze shuddered through the field. After the woman brushed the hair from her face, she saw a fully formed creature before her. It towered above her, like some nightmare from an ancient myth, as mud and stones and worms fell off of its limbs. The rising sun behind the woman reflected off two gleaming rocks in the figure that could easily have been mistaken for eyes.

Mara smiled. "Greetings, old friend," she said.

# 16

Zak woke up in a panic. "Mom! Dad! Where are you?!" he cried.

He threw off an unfamiliar blanket and stared up in confusion at a high, vaulted ceiling. The room was shaped like an octagon. Four of the sides were covered with floor-to-ceiling windows. Three sides were covered with tall bookshelves. A heavy door in the last wall was sealed shut.

It took a few long moments before Zak realized where he was. *That's right,* he remembered. *I'm in Dr. Hoo's library.*

Stiffly, Zak rose up from the sofa he had been sleeping on. He was still wearing the jeans and shirt from the night before. They were dirty and torn, with several spots of dried blood on his shirt.

Zak shuddered. *I'll never forget those things that attacked us last night,* he thought. *I still can't believe it really happened.*

Just then, the door pushed open with a slow creak. Zak twitched nervously.

"You're finally awake!" said a small blond girl.

Zak let out a sigh of relief. "Louise," he said. "Where is everybody?"

"Me and Dr. Hoo are eating breakfast," she said, as if it were the most normal thing in the world. "He asked me to come check on you."

"But what about Pablo and Thora?" Zak asked. "Where are they?"

"They stopped the trolls out in the field," Louise announced proudly.

"So, they're still gone?" Zak asked.

Louise nodded. She looked calm, happy, and at ease. *Great,* thought Zak. *A little kid is handling all of this better than I am.*

Suddenly, Louise's eyebrows shot up. She ran past

Zak and pounced on the sofa. "There you are!" she exclaimed.

Nestled within the folds of Zak's blanket was a small brown and white bunny. "I looked for you all night," Louise said, nuzzling it.

She turned to Zak. "Did you find him?" she asked gleefully. "Thank you so much!" Louise hugged Zak around the shoulders. The bunny's soft ears tickled Zak's chin as she hugged him.

Zak shook his head. He felt dizzy and confused. A dull pain ached in his head. He felt blood crusted under a nostril.

"The doctor said you were in a car accident," said Louise, playing with her pet.

"How did you know that?" Zak muttered.

"After the trolls were gone, you sat down on the sofa and fell asleep," said Louise. "You kept mumbling about your mom and dad."

"Oh," Zak said, finding it hard to focus. A buzzing sound seemed to be slowly filling his head.

Louise ran to a window. "Buzz, buzz," she said.

Zak walked up next to her and looked out. The

buzzing was coming from outside. Dark, glistening clouds spiraled into long funnels.

"Look at all those flies!" cried Louise.

Louise was right. The clouds were, in fact, twisting swarms of insects. Thousands of them. They flew past the house to the south, following County Road One.

"Where are they going?" asked Louise.

"No idea," said Zak. He heard more buzzing. He lowered his gaze to see several large houseflies banging themselves against the glass. Zak flipped the latch and opened the window. The insects zoomed off to join the swarm.

"Cool!" cried Louise.

*I think I'm gonna be sick,* thought Zak.

Louise turned away from the window. Still holding her bunny, she grabbed one of Zak's arms with her free hand and pulled him toward the door. "Come on," she said. "You look hungry!"

# 17

From the edge of the field, Thora and Pablo could see Dr. Hoo's house. "It looks taller from this side," Thora said.

"I know," said Pablo. "It's weird, but I swear it was only two stories yesterday, but we walked up four flights of stairs."

They walked along the line of trees that marked the boundary between the field and the doctor's overgrown yard. Above them, the highest tree branches blocked the sunlight from above.

Thora shivered in the shadows. She glanced around the yard, taking it all in. The scraggly bushes next to the house reminded her of crouching trolls —

like the one that had sung to her in the woods. The knobby, leafless branches looked like the arms that had reached for her.

*Are the trolls really gone?* she wondered.

Next to the edge of Dr. Hoo's house was a tall bush that still had most of its leaves. It stood as tall as a man and swayed gently in the breeze. There was a strange, shifting shadow on the other side of it.

Suddenly, she heard a whisper. *Thora . . . don't forget me . . .*

"What did you say?" Thora asked Pablo.

Pablo frowned. "I didn't say anything," he said. "Oh, you mean about the house?"

"No," Thora said. "Did you say something after that?"

"Nope," Pablo said. He narrowed his eyes at her. "Are you feeling okay?"

The sunlight was inching farther down the branches of the trees. Soon, the sun would be creeping above the roof. But the dark and gloomy bush seemed to be growing darker and larger.

*Thora . . . I'm hungry . . .*

"You're hungry?" Thora asked Pablo.

"I guess," said Pablo. "Are you?"

*I need your help . . .*

Thora swung her head left and right. *It's not Pablo's voice,* she realized.

It felt like whispers were coming from all around her. Cold shivers ran up and down Thora's spine. "Where's the door?" she asked, her voice cracking.

"What?" said Pablo.

Thora ran past Pablo and rushed toward the house. "The door!" Thora repeated. "The bushes are blocking the door!"

A thick barrier of intertwined branches and vines had risen between them and the front door.

"Thora, wait!" Pablo cried. But she was already worming her way through the bushes, shoving branches aside. Twigs snapped. Vines dragged behind her, seemingly sucking her in.

Pablo pushed himself in, following her path. Vines clung to his shirt and his jeans. Pablo pulled them off hastily.

The bushes grew thicker and darker the farther

they ventured. With each branch they pushed aside, more whipped back at them.

"How much farther is it?" called Pablo.

Thora put her head down and kept shoving. At one point, the branches grew so thick that they seemed to block out all light.

*Thora . . . Thora . . .*

*No,* she thought. *I won't listen to it!*

Thora's arms were scratched and bleeding, but she kept pushing forward, ripping vines from her arms and legs as she moved. Finally, she emerged on the other side, scraped and bloody. She let out a sigh of relief.

"Thora!" cried Pablo's voice. "Help!"

"Take my arm!" Thora said.

She extended her small white hand through the webbed branches. She felt a strong tug on her hand and pulled Pablo through the dark and into the light.

Pablo leaned against the wall, panting from the effort. The door stood a few feet away. "Are you okay?" he asked.

"I'm — I'm just tired," Thora said. "And hungry."

"Me too," said Pablo.

As Pablo closed the door behind them, Thora noticed a darker shape within the twigs and branches. It looked like a shadow that formed the outline of a person.

*Thora . . . Thora . . . Thora!*

"Thora?" Pablo said. She looked at Pablo and saw a silver light shining in his eyes. At that moment, the whispers stopped.

Without saying a word, Pablo led Thora into the house, toward the welcoming aroma of fried eggs and bacon.

# 18

Bryce Gamble was no longer lying on the ground in the forest. Somehow, after what seemed like centuries, he had pulled away from the vines and grass. Slowly, he had crawled to the edge of the forest where he saw a house in the distance.

It felt like months had passed since he'd been separated from Thora in the forest. They'd been looking for Louise, and lost sight of each other.

*Food,* he thought. *I must have food.*

Hunger pushed Bryce onward. He trudged closer to the house. Each step felt as if his feet had turned to rock. He stopped to catch his breath by the corner of the house.

The sun was rising higher. The light stung his face and hands. He wished he could hide from the light.

Suddenly, a shadow covered his limbs. It formed around his body like a second skin, cooling him. Calming him. The darkness around him grew deeper and thicker. He felt safe and protected now. He also felt stronger.

Then Bryce heard voices. A girl and a boy, walking together, talking. They were heading toward the house. Toward him.

*Thora . . .*

Thora glanced around, but kept walking.

Bryce tried to call Thora's name, but his lips wouldn't move. Shadows shaped like vines were wrapped around his mouth and face, changing him . . .

*Thora . . . help me . . .*

*Why doesn't she stop?* Bryce thought. *It must be Pablo's fault. Yes, it's all his fault.*

Pablo and Thora were talking to each other. Bryce couldn't understand the words they were speaking. It sounded like another language. But Bryce knew Pablo was taking Thora away. Stealing her.

*No!* Bryce thought. *I won't let him!*

Now Thora was running. Bryce had to stop them. Something made him feel like it was important to prevent them from entering that house.

*I'm so hungry . . .*

*Why don't they see me?* Bryce wondered. He tried to grab them. It took all of his willpower to grasp onto Pablo's clothes and arms. The shadow clinging to Bryce made it seem like Pablo was passing right through him. The darkness surrounding Bryce was so thick now that he could barely see at all.

Before Bryce knew it, the two had passed him. They were entering the door!

*Thora,* thought Bryce. *Thora . . . Thora!*

Bryce watched Pablo lead Thora inside. He slammed the door shut behind them.

A wild hatred boiled inside of Bryce. Pablo had taken Thora away. Bryce felt his hunger grow even stronger. *He must be destroyed,* Bryce thought. *I must eat.*

Like an old oak with deep roots, Bryce waited patiently for the boy to return.

Hours crawled by, but Bryce did not move. The shadow swarmed around him, keeping him safe from the dangerous sunlight. It whispered comfortable, familiar things to him.

Then Bryce realized something. *If Pablo does return, how can I stop him? It's hard for me to even move. And he's so fast.*

Then Bryce felt the presence of others behind him. He turned, slowly, to see that the yard was filling up with other shadows. Other people. Or were they simply more bushes that he hadn't noticed before?

He saw dark, shadowy forms within the bushes. Several men, a woman, a child. The shadows slithered and shifted. Bryce couldn't see their faces, but he knew they were his friends. They would wait with him.

They would help him.

# 19

Mara walked confidently across the field. Following close behind her, like a crooked shadow, was the hulking troll. It lumbered heavily through the tall grass as they approached the Nye farm. As they neared the house, Mara noticed its peeling paint, missing roof shingles, and broken windows.

*It looks abandoned,* Mara thought. Still, she walked up to the front door and knocked. Uzhk, her troll companion, stood silently behind her.

After no one answered, Mara knocked again. "Hello," she called. "Anyone there?"

No response came. "Hello," Mara said again. "I'm Mara Lovecraft. We spoke on the phone last week."

Mara put her face up to the door's window and peered in. "What a mess," she mumbled to her companion. "I don't know how anyone lives out here in the middle of nowhere."

A grunt escaped the creature's lips.

Mara walked to the rear of the house. She saw an SUV sitting in the driveway that curved up behind the house. The front end was smashed in. The hood was missing and the windshield was shattered. Two of the tires were gone, too. But what made Mara shiver were the deep scratches along one side of the car.

Scratches made by gigantic claws.

"Do you think someone's been here recently, Uzhk?" she asked, looking over her shoulder. The creature slowly nodded.

Mara approached the car. There were gouges in the dirt behind the vehicle. *Something dragged it to this spot,* she realized. In front of the car was more of the tall, dry grass. *No tow truck brought the car here,* Mara thought. *Otherwise, there would be tracks from the truck leading through the grass.*

"Come on," Mara said, motioning for Uzhk to follow.

The strange companions headed toward a large, rusty silo in the distance. A moment later, Uzhk reached out a massive hand and touched Mara's shoulder.

"What is it?" Mara asked.

The creature cocked its head as if it were listening to a distant sound. Mara nodded. She heard it now, too — a sound like a strong breeze. But when she looked back at the trees, she saw that there was no wind.

But next to the house, the grass and weeds were bent low, creating a channel that headed directly toward her. The overgrown yard looked like a quiet lagoon with an invisible alligator swimming through it.

"*Thyul hu*," growled Uzhk.

"Snakes," Mara agreed.

A river of shiny scales and darting tongues emerged into the open. Mara hopped onto the rear fender of the wrecked car. The troll looked amused by the countless snakes that swarmed around his feet. Something vaguely resembling a smile appeared on

Uzhk's face. Mara had read that trolls couldn't smile. It had something to do with the anatomy of their skulls and the lack of muscles in their faces.

Of course, Uzhk was a *drakhool*, different from the larger, more ruthless *gathool*. The two species of trolls were natural enemies. The *drakhool* believed in leaving humans alone — not in enslaving or eating them.

The reptiles continued to move, ignoring Mara and Uzhk. All of them moved with a single mind, like a net of living ropes gliding across the grass. Mara saw they were heading to the same destination: the silo.

Mara leapt off the car and followed them. She and Uzhk ran to the curving wall of the rusted tower. The serpents rushed forward, hurling themselves through the door and into the dark pit inside.

Uzhk bent down, preparing to follow the slithering horde down into the chasm. Mara stopped him, shaking her head. "We need help," she said.

The young woman pulled her phone from a pocket. *If Dr. Hoo was right,* she thought, *then we'll need a lot of help.*

Uzkh suddenly groaned, putting his hands to his ears as a monstrous hiss echoed through the silo. A vast number of serpent throats sounded a collective cry from deep down in the pit. Mara couldn't tell whether the snakes were frightened or overjoyed, but something had surprised them inside that building.

And Mara had a terrible feeling that she knew what it was.

# 20

After breakfast, Dr. Hoo led Thora, Pablo, Zak, and Louise back upstairs to the library. "There's something all of you must see," he said.

Dr. Hoo burst through the door at the top of the stairs and hurried to the center of his library. White clouds and blue sky greeted them through all four windows. Sunlight streamed across the floor and lit up a wooden stand. A large book on top was already open. Dr. Hoo approached it and flipped through pages. "We'll find what we need in here," he said.

The aged pages were covered with colorful paintings of stars and constellations. One painting showed a half-horse, half-man holding a bow and arrow.

"That looks like the centaur we saw in the woods!" said Pablo.

Dr. Hoo looked at him and grinned. "Exactly," he said. "He's also known as Sagittarius."

He turned the page, revealing two young men standing side by side. They held long swords in their hands.

"That's the Gemini constellation," said Thora, tilting her head. "We learned about the zodiac in astronomy class."

The doctor turned the page again. The next painting showed a beautiful woman wearing a crown. She held a large stone jar above her head. A strange liquid poured out from it like a brilliant shower of stars.

"Aquarius?" asked Thora. "But I thought it was supposed to be a man."

"Not always," said the doctor. "It is said that the water in her magical cup can preserve life, or snuff it out."

"She's pretty," whispered Louise.

Zak threw his hands up. "What's the deal?" he

asked. "Why are we looking at pictures of some stupid stars?"

"They're more than just stars," said Dr. Hoo. "Just as the legends about trolls are real, so are the legends behind the constellations."

"What do you mean?" asked Thora. "How is any of this going to help us?"

"Be patient," Dr. Hoo scolded, turning another page. "You'll have your answers shortly."

The next page showed a huge constellation of a twisting serpent. Its long body was coiled in seven silver knots. "The Draco constellation," Dr. Hoo said. "The meteor shower last night was called the Draconid shower, because it looked like the meteors came from Draco."

The doctor flipped another page. It showed the silhouette of a ferocious beast traced against a backdrop of stars.

"A bear!" cried Louise.

"The Great Bear," Dr. Hoo said. He looked across the book toward Zak. "Also known as Ursa Major."

The doctor turned one more page, showing them

a painting of a young, bearded warrior holding a club in one hand and a lion's head in the other.

"Orion," Pablo said without hesitation. Dr. Hoo nodded at him.

"We're wasting time," growled Zak. "We need to find my parents."

"And my brother," Thora added, crossing her arms.

"I understand," Dr. Hoo said, "but there's more. The legends of many ancient peoples tell of a huge battle. A war between the powers of darkness and the powers of light. Many ancient texts tell the story of an ancient dragon who fought with the stars in the sky."

Thora's eyes brightened. "Falling stars?" she repeated. "You know, during the meteor shower last night . . . I swear I saw a star fall from Orion's belt."

"Perhaps you did," the doctor answered. He leaned closer. "Perhaps the ancient stories describe a real, true war," he suggested. "A war between creatures of darkness and beings of light. That battle may still be going on. And the trolls, emerging from deep below the surface, may have begun a new war."

Silence swept over the room, each person lost in

thought. Wind rattled the library windows. Moving trees threw shadows across the ancient pages of the book.

Zak finally broke the silence. "That doesn't help me find my mom and dad," he said. "Where are they, Doc?"

Dr. Hoo stared down at the desk. "I'm not sure," he said. "But I know that by defeating these creatures, we stand a better chance of finding your parents. And your brother, Thora."

Thora squinted. "If everything you're saying is true," she said, "then how can the stars help us?"

Dr. Hoo grinned. He opened his mouth to speak, but just then, a few musical notes chimed out. The doctor pulled his phone from beneath his cape. As he moved away and spoke in hushed tones, the rest of them leafed through the book.

Zak rubbed his forehead, visibly upset. "These star things, these constellations," he said. "Is he trying to tell us they're, like, real people? That they're on Earth right now?"

"Stars aren't people," Thora said sternly. "They're

gigantic balls of gas and chemicals. The closest star is light-years away. Even if someone could travel at the speed of light, it would take years to get here."

"Are you sure about that?" Dr. Hoo said. He clicked his phone shut and returned it to the folds of his cape. "The entire universe is made of the same basic matter, the same atoms. All of us were originally made from stardust."

Dr. Hoo walked back to the book. He placed his hands on the volume, turning one last page as he spoke. "Perhaps the old astrologers were trying, in a superstitious way, to explain the connection between us and the stars," he said. "After all, what ancient people used to call magic eventually became known as science. Lightning wasn't a magical weapon thrown by Zeus — it was electricity."

No one spoke for a moment. Everyone, even the doctor, seemed to be lost in their thoughts — and in the pages of the book.

After a moment, Louise piped up. "Who was on the phone?" she asked.

"That was a colleague of mine," said the doctor.

He pointed at the broad shelf behind him. "She's the one who gave me those books about the *gathool* that I showed you last night. And now she needs our help."

Zak's eyes narrowed. "What kind of help?"

"She's found where the trolls are planning to attack next," said the doctor. "And if we can't stop them, all of Zion Falls will be destroyed."

# 21

Dr. Hoo hurried Thora, Louise, Zak, and Pablo down a long passageway that ended in a heavy metal door. He opened seven different locks.

"Why don't we just go out the front?" asked Pablo.

"The other entrance is . . . too dangerous right now," the doctor said.

Dr. Hoo pulled the door open with a powerful tug. His SUV was parked a few feet away.

As they all left the building, Dr. Hoo reached inside his cape and pulled out a set of keys. He tossed them to Zak, who nimbly caught them.

"Do any of you know where the old Nye farm is?" Dr. Hoo asked. "The one with the big silo?"

"I know where it is," said Pablo.

"Good," said the doctor. "Show Zak how to get there."

Dr. Hoo opened the SUV's rear door and ushered Louise and Thora inside. "Please hurry," Dr. Hoo said. "Mara needs your help. It should only take you a few minutes to get there."

"Aren't you coming with us?" asked Thora.

The doctor didn't answer. He was staring back at the trees and bushes surrounding his house. Although the sun had risen higher, the shadows were deeper around the old stone building.

The doctor turned back to face them. Pablo looked intently at his swirling cape. Although Pablo still couldn't see within the cape's shadows, he was saw something move beneath its folds. A third arm. He was sure of it.

"Mara's waiting for you," Dr. Hoo said. "Now hurry. I'll be there as soon as I can."

Zak roared the engine to life. As the doctor waved goodbye, the SUV bounced down the dirt driveway. Then they turned east onto County Road One.

Pablo pointed out a dirt path up ahead. "That's the road to the Nye farm," he told Zak.

Zak stomped on the accelerator. The SUV zoomed right past the dirt path.

"Zak, where are you going?" asked Thora. "Turn around — right now!"

"Hold on," said Zak. "I need to do something first."

A few miles down the road, Zak finally hit the brakes. There, in the center of the road, some pieces of a car were scattered on the asphalt. Two tires lay on their sides. A crumbled, detached hood rested between them. The remains of a windshield were scattered across the road from one side to the other.

Zak jumped out of the SUV. "It's gone," he said softly.

Pablo turned to Thora and Louise in the back seat. "This is where Zak's family had the accident," Pablo explained. "I saw the car. It was right there."

Pablo, Thora, and Louise all climbed out of the car. Slowly, they walked toward Zak.

"Maybe they towed it away," Thora suggested.

Pablo shook his head. "Then why did they leave all this junk here?" he asked.

Zak stared at the scattered glass and debris. "Someone took it," he said. "Some *thing* took the whole car!"

Louise pulled her rabbit closer. "The big bad wolf," she whispered.

"Let's get back in the car, Zak," Pablo said. "I think the doctor was right — if we help his friend Mara stop these trolls, then we'll be able to find your folks."

"And Bryce," added Thora.

Zak spun to face them. "Us? Help?" he growled. "This is a job for the cops, the National Guard, or something!"

Pablo faced the open road and spread his arms out. "Look at the road," he said. "Do any of you see anything weird?"

"You mean besides my dad's missing car?" said Zak.

"The accident was last night," said Pablo. "We've been gone for, what, eighteen hours? So why didn't anyone else move this debris? It covers the road."

"So?" asked Thora.

"So," said Pablo, "that means no one has traveled on this road since then. Where are the police? What about people driving to school, or to work? And listen to how quiet it is."

Everyone craned their necks to listen. Not one bird sang. Not a single horsefly hummed. All the sounds of a normal October afternoon were missing.

"We might not be the only ones who came across trolls last night," Pablo added.

Pablo's comment made Thora glance nervously at the nearby trees. "Let's get in the car, Louise," she said, leading the girl by the shoulder.

"Yeah," agreed Pablo. "Let's get out of here."

Zak shook his head. Dark shadows lined the front of his face.

"Zak," Pablo said. "The doctor gave you the keys. He's counting on us. His friend needs our help."

Zak let out a deep sigh. He looked over at Pablo, then straightened up with a jerk.

"Pablo," Zak said, "your eyes look . . . weird."

"What? Mine?" said Pablo.

"Yeah," said Zak. "Shiny. Like stars. You're not going to turn into a zombie or something, are you?"

Pablo grinned. "We're hunting trolls, not zombies."

Zak smirked. "Oh yeah. What was I thinking?" he said. "Zombies aren't real."

Everyone laughed — except Thora. Her face was as white as a sheet. She lifted a finger to point behind the others.

When they turned, they saw the entire SUV was crawling with giant, croaking toads.

# 22

As the SUV disappeared down his gravel driveway, Dr. Hoo felt a cold shadow envelop his body. But unlike most autumn shadows that came down from above, this shadow came up from below. A strange mist was seeping out of the ground.

The doctor had been waiting for this to happen. The natural surroundings were being affected by the trolls' return to the surface. Vegetation, animal life, the weather — they were all beginning to fall under the control of the *gathool*, under the growing influence of their evil presence.

Icy coldness grasped the doctor's feet and legs. Mist swirled around his body like a creeping vine.

Dr. Hoo closed his eyes and concentrated. Being frightened by the dark mist would only make it harder to resist. Instead, the doctor thought about the young heroes in his SUV. They would eventually need his help. He had to be strong for them.

Slowly, he pulled his left foot off the ground. Then his right. It felt like he was walking through thick mud. Each and every step took great effort.

When Dr. Hoo finally reached his house, his shirt was soaked in sweat. He shut the door behind him and turned all seven locks. Then he pressed his face to the small-paned window. He saw bushes flailing back and forth outside. But there had been no wind just a moment ago.

Dr. Hoo started down the passageway back to his library, his head hung low from exhaustion. Weakened, he slowly trudged up the stairs. As he entered the library, he heard a gravelly voice.

"Doctor?"

Dr. Hoo raised his gaze to see a young man blocking his path. Wet leaves clung to his clothes and his uncombed hair. His eyes glittered darkly behind a pair of cracked glasses. The boy was completely still, except for his twitching fingers at the ends of his long, skinny arms.

"Bryce?" Dr. Hoo asked uncertainly. "Is that you?"

The boy clenched his fists. Dr. Hoo saw that he held a pocket knife in one of them.

"Doctor," the young man repeated, his voice cold and hard. "Where is Thora?"

# 23

"Gun it, Zak!" yelled Pablo.

"I can't see the road!" Zak cried. He flipped on the windshield wipers, but they couldn't move the squat, sticky bodies of the countless toads.

"Just turn us around!" said Pablo.

Zak slammed the SUV into reverse. The tires squealed against the asphalt as the vehicle whipped to the side. The sickening splats of squished toads sounded from below their seats.

"Yuck," said Louise.

The SUV raced down the road, but the view was still blocked. Zak looked out the window. Countless wet toads were slapping softly onto the asphalt.

"They're falling from the sky!" Thora cried out.

"Hold on!" yelled Zak. He swerved the SUV back and forth. The movement rocked his passengers from side to side, but it also flipped some of the toads off the front of the vehicle.

"The turn isn't far from here," Pablo announced.

Five more fat toads plopped onto the windshield. Zak spun the steering wheel back and forth, jerking the SUV around violently. Louise screamed.

"Why did we bring her?" asked Zak. "We should have taken her home."

"I don't have a home," whimpered Louise.

"It burned down," explained Thora.

Zak frowned. "I'm sorry," he said, "but she's just a kid. She might get hurt."

Louise pulled herself up and leaned over the front seat. "I can help," she said. "I hit that one troll with my flare gun." To make her point, she pulled the flare pistol from her pocket and waved it confidently in Zak's face.

"She did save Thora," said Pablo. "That troll might have gotten her if not for Louise."

Zak clenched his teeth. "Okay, okay," he said. "Just don't let her fire that thing in here."

Louise plopped back down next to Thora in the back seat. "I'm not a child," Louise muttered. Thora chuckled and pulled the girl close.

"There's the road!" yelled Pablo.

Zak gripped the wheel and made a hard left. The SUV flew off the asphalt and onto a dusty dirt road. The bumps and ruts threw several more toads off the vehicle. Only a few still managed to cling to the hood as the vehicle bounced wildly over the bumpy terrain.

Pablo pointed his shaking arm toward the front of the car. "I can see the Nye farm up ahead," he said.

A moment later, the SUV squealed to a halt next to the old house. "That's my parents' car," Zak said grimly. "What's it doing here?"

# 24

Everyone piled out of the SUV and raced over to Zak's parents' car. Zak ran his fingers along the deep scratches along the sides. He looked up, dazed, at Pablo. "Trolls?" he asked.

Pablo nodded grimly.

"Over here!" came a voice from behind. A young woman jogged up to greet them. She wore dark jeans tucked into a pair of muddy boots. A black ponytail hung over the collar of her long coat.

"I'm Mara Lovecraft," she said. "Dr. Hoo sent you all here, right?"

Thora nodded. "But I don't know how we can help you."

"I have a flare gun," said Louise, holding up her weapon.

Mara glanced at the little girl with a confused look on her face.

"The doctor said you figured out where the trolls were going to attack next," said Pablo.

Mara's face lit up with surprise. "Orion," she said.

Pablo squinted. "How did you know my last name?" he asked.

"Last name?" said Mara. "I don't. I mean, I . . . didn't the doctor tell you?"

Zak took a step forward. "Tell us what?" he demanded.

"I've been trying to call him," Mara said, "but he isn't answering his phone. It's not like him to ignore my calls."

"What was the doctor supposed to tell us?" Zak repeated.

"How you can help," Mara said. "How all of you can help. Hurry, come with me!"

Mara led them to the rusty silo. A huge, gaping hole had been ripped in its side. Hundreds of toads and frogs were hurling themselves through the doorway and into the dark pit inside. A loud hissing sound echoed inside the silo.

"What's with all these creatures?!" cried Zak. "There must be thousands of them!"

"The trolls — the *gathool* — are entering our world," said Mara. "They are sending up their own ship from deep within the earth."

"What kind of ship?" asked Thora.

"It's called the *bazhargak*, or Dark Tower," said Mara. "The best way to describe it is a moving castle. A huge building filled with hundreds of *gathool*. That's why the reptiles and amphibians — their servants — are here. They've come to help the tower rise to the surface."

A tremor shook the ground.

"It's coming!" said Mara. "The Dark Tower's highest point will pierce through the ground and rise up through this silo. The *gathool* picked this site so no one would see them arrive . . . until it was too late."

Another tremor ran through the farmyard. A loud metallic shriek sounded from deep within the silo.

"Can it be stopped?" asked Pablo.

Mara shook her head weakly. "I don't know."

"Then why did the doctor send us here?" Zak yelled. "What's this got to do with getting my parents back? Why isn't Dr. Hoo here to help?!"

A harsh groan forced them all to look upward. The silo was swaying, tilting, and grinding against its cement foundation. Zak walked up next to the pit and stared deep down into the blackness. "I see it!"

The others crept closer to the edge of the pit. The wide rounded tunnel plunged straight into the heart of the earth. A few hundred feet below lay a slick green bulb. It reminded Thora of a gigantic acorn squash. Except this squash was a hundred times larger and had pale green spikes growing from the center. Slimy black tentacles waved around its sides. They were covered with red suckers that shone wetly in the dim light. It was rising quickly.

"That's only the tip of the tower," Mara said. "The entry gate is near the bottom. That's where the troll army will exit. If that happens, our world is doomed."

Suddenly, the top of the green squash split open

like a pus-filled wound. A dark figure forced its way up, climbing through the slimy mass. He perched himself atop of the rising shape, his gigantic muscles tensed, preparing for battle.

"A troll!" shouted Zak. "A big one!"

"The doctor should be here," whispered Mara.

Suddenly, a dark cloud rose from the fields and surrounded the silo like a thick, black curtain hovering in the air. Then, with alarming speed, darkness surrounded them on all sides.

Everything went black.

# 25

Flies. Countless flies.

They swarmed around the silo, circling like a tornado made of insect wings and night. Flies buzzed in their ears, crawled in their hair, and swept across their eyes.

"The flies are blocking out the light!" Mara cried. "I can't see anything!"

"We have to stop —" Pablo began, then he gagged. He spat out a mouthful of insects. "We have to stop them!"

More tremors rocked the earth. The silo's metal tore away from the concrete base. Louise dropped her rabbit. It disappeared into the furious swarm.

Pablo's mind raced. Blurred thoughts came quickly. *How?* he thought. *How can we do anything?* He and Thora had come up with a plan to outrun the trolls last night. But they couldn't run from this.

Dr. Hoo had said that the stories of the warrior constellations were real. *As real as trolls,* Pablo remembered. *But if that's true, then where are they now?*

Pablo tried to think of a solution. He knew that sunlight would destroy a troll, but even though an afternoon sun blazed somewhere in the sky, the curtain of flies was creating its own nighttime. They were shielding the monstrous troll at the tip of the tower from the damaging sunlight.

For some reason, Pablo recalled the starlight he saw in Zak's eyes earlier. Zak had said Pablo's eyes shone, too. *Are we really warriors from the stars?* Pablo thought. It was all jumbled up in his head. *Starlight. Constellations. Magic. Science.*

Pablo heard the roaring grow louder in his left ear. But the sound was different now. It was deeper, like a growl. He opened his eyes and almost screamed.

Pablo had expected to see Zak standing next to him. Instead, a giant silver bear was growling wildly amidst the insect swarm!

It raised its thick, furry arm above its head. Pablo couldn't believe his eyes as the tremendous, hairy paw swiped at the flies. With each sweep of its massive arm, hundreds of flies fell lifelessly to the ground. Not only the bear's swipes, but its silver light also seemed to be damaging the buzzing swarm.

*It's Zak!* Pablo realized.

Pablo called out to the bear, but his voice sounded deeper. Older. He looked down and saw huge weapons in his hands. Then he saw that his clothes had changed. An ornate metal breastplate covered his chest. A thick kilt of leather strips protected his thighs. His feet were no longer bare, either. Instead, he was wearing sandals. He was dressed like an ancient Roman warrior!

Pablo instinctively swung his weapons back and forth, spilling silver light along the arc of his weapons' paths. Flies fell by the hundreds at each blow.

Pablo and the silver bear fought side by side, their

brilliant light radiated into the swarm, burning away at its center.

*Where are Thora and Louise?* Pablo wondered. He turned to his right and saw two young women dressed in flowing silver robes. They resembled his two friends, but they also looked like the zodiac images in Dr. Hoo's book.

The taller girl was trying to lift an ornate jar of gleaming light off of the ground. The jar vibrated with energy. She lifted with all her might, but couldn't lift the jar past her waist. Her arms shook as she tried to raise it above her head.

"I can't lift it!" Thora's voice cried out from the woman's lips. "It's too heavy!"

Louise stepped forward. She reached up and braced the jar with her small, silver hand. Immediately it glowed brighter.

Up and up, Louise helped Thora lift the jar. Slowly but surely, they lifted it over Thora's head.

Suddenly, a flood of molten silver gushed out of the jar like water out of a burst dam. Wave after wave of silver liquid spilled into the pit.

The silver liquid beat down against the rising tower. The brilliant liquid streamed impossibly from the jar without slowing. Its flow also splashed against the swarming insects, pushing them back.

The hunter and the bear kept batting at the flies. The insects fell at their sandaled or hairy feet. Thora and Louise kept the jar held high. Soon, the flood had filled most of the deep tunnel with a silvery liquid. The slimy green top of the tower sat just above the water level, like a rotten lily pad on a silver pond. It was still rising.

Pablo could see the troll at the tip of the tower. He was only a few hundred feet from the surface now. The troll braced himself against the flood, managing to hang on despite its rushing force.

But the tower continued to rise. Its black tentacles waved furiously as they pulled the tower closer and closer to the surface.

Then the earth began to tremble. This time, it wasn't the Dark Tower that shook the ground. The women's jar was gleaming brighter and brighter. It blazed like a small, silver-white star.

"It's too hot!" shouted Thora.

"Don't worry," came Louise's voice. "I can help." She touched the jar with her silver hand again. The gleaming light began to flow out of the jar!

Small stars began to surge out from the jar. They filled the silo with brilliant light. One shooting star struck the troll and knocked him off the tower. The monster tumbled down, down, disappearing into the shining, silver lake.

"YES!" cried Thora.

But soaring through the flame and smoke, the evil tower still rose. Thora choked and coughed on the bitter fumes.

"Don't stop now!" cried Louise's voice.

The groaning in the silo grew louder. The ground shook. The insect swarm tightened its circle around the companions. But the fiery stream kept pouring from the jar, and the two warriors kept up their attack.

Thora heard a screech echo within the metal silo. It grew loud as thunder, then suddenly faded as the stampede of flies rushed away.

Something was happening to the tower. Its circle of tentacles, blackened and charred, no longer waved. The tower's ascent was slowing down.

The four warriors gasped as the tower creaked its way up past the surface. It came to a stop as the tip of the tower scraped against the roof of the silo. At once, the starlight that had surrounded the warriors faded, and their bodies changed back to their normal forms.

Suddenly, a ball of flame formed at the tip of the tower. "Get back!" shouted Mara.

All of them dashed out of the hole in the side of the silo. A black cloud billowed upward as a massive explosion burst outward. They could feel the force of the blast against their backs.

The rusty building blazed like a torch as the roof flew off, followed by the silo in entirety. Then, with a sudden gasp of wind, a giant flame rocketed into the sky.

Pablo and the others were violently hurled to the ground.

The five of them crawled quickly away from the fire, coughing and spitting out insects.

A hot wind swept over their sweat-stained faces. The orange and gold inferno blazed in their eyes. For a few moments, they all stared at the remains of the rusty tower.

Thora slowly stood. "Did we stop it?" she asked.

Pablo walked over to touch the silver fluid that had filled the pit. It had solidified into a hard metallic element and felt cold to the touch. "Nothing's coming through here anymore!" he said excitedly.

Mara nodded and smiled. "Yes," she said. "The *bazhargak* has been stopped. The trolls will not be able to enter our world from here."

Zak fell into a sitting position upon the ground. "Did that really just happen?" he said to no one in particular.

"Yep!" Louise said cheerily. She walked over to him and held out her hand. "You turned into a grizzly bear and scared away the big bad wolf."

Zak grinned. He took Louise's hand and stood, making sure to pretend the much smaller girl was helping him get to his feet. "You did pretty well yourself, kid," he told Louise.

"Really?" Louise asked, her eyes bright. "Did I really help?"

Thora smiled at Louise. "Really," she said, nodding her head.

Zak mussed up Louise's hair. "How's it feel to be a hero, kid?" he teased.

Louise smiled and giggled.

Pablo suddenly hooted, clapping Zak on the back. "That was awesome, man!" Pablo said. "I still can't believe you turned into a bear!"

. "Speak for yourself," Zak said. "The way you were swinging those weapons, you looked like a Roman gladiator, or something."

Pablo laughed. Then he pointed at Thora proudly. "And what about her jar?" he said.

Zak smiled. "Yeah, that was pretty sweet, too," he admitted.

As Thora beamed with pride, Pablo noticed a glint of light flickering in her eyes. Then, for a moment, her eyes met Pablo's. She looked away and began to blush. Pablo shuffled his feet and stared at the ground.

Louise leaped between them, then started jumping up and down excitedly. "And the silver dress I wore!" she cried. "It was so pretty."

Zak just laughed. "You looked like . . . like . . ."

"Like Libra," finished Pablo. "Louise is Libra. She holds the scales, balancing the sides. She turns the tide."

Louise smiled.

Mara nodded her head. "Without Louise's power of balance," she said, "your other powers would not have been enough. Like individual stars in one constellation, each of you played an important part in this victory."

Mara stepped closer to stand between the four young heroes. "And I have a feeling you'll all play an important role in the battle to come."

The four companions were silent as they weighed the meaning of Mara's words. After a moment, Thora broke the silence. "You looked like Orion, Pablo," she said. "Like your last name."

*Orion. O'Ryan. That's what Mara said to me earlier,* thought Pablo. *She recognized me as Orion, the hunter.*

"Maybe Dr. Hoo was right," Pablo said. "Maybe we are the heroes from the stars!"

"We should go tell Dr. Hoo all about what happened," Thora suggested.

Mara smiled. "That's a great idea."

"And Dr. Hoo will know what we should do next," Mara added.

And with that, they all piled into the SUV and drove toward Dr. Hoo's house.

# 26

The SUV bounced along the rutted driveway. Its headlights waved up and down with each bump. Its horn honked cheerfully as they arrived outside Dr. Hoo's house. The shadows were shorter now, and more light seemed to shine through the trees.

Mara and the young heroes leaped out of the SUV. For a brief moment, they watched the tip of the fiery tower blaze in the distance like a bright orange finger pointing skyward. Black smoke billowed from the tip and merged with the gray clouds overhead.

They rushed to the door and hurried inside. They were excited to share the good news with Dr. Hoo.

"Doctor!" Mara yelled. "The kids have done it! Where are you?"

They ran through the entire house yelling for the doctor, but their cries went unanswered. Their footsteps echoed through the halls as they rushed toward the library.

Thora peeked around the corner of the door, fully expecting to see Dr. Hoo at the desk studying ancient tomes or astronomical texts. Instead, the room lay dark and silent. At that moment, their lively voices dwindled into silence.

"He's not here," whispered Mara. "Why isn't he here?"

Just then, Thora spotted a long, dark cloak laying on the floor. She picked it up. "It's Dr. Hoo's cape," she said quietly.

As she lifted the cloak, Thora saw there was an object underneath. "That's Bryce's pocket knife," she said. "What is this doing here?"

Pablo knelt down next to Thora. He pressed his fingers into a dark splotch upon the floor a short distance from where the cape lay.

"Is this . . . blood?" Pablo asked quietly.

Mara looked down at Pablo's fingers. "Yes," she said somberly.

Louise pointed at the wall above the pool of blood. "What does that word mean?" she asked.

Thora followed her finger. A word had been crudely carved into the wooden wall a few feet above the floor.

It read: CROATOAN.

Thora's heart sank. The word had been carved with a pocket knife. Bryce's knife. "What does 'croatoan' mean?" Thora asked.

Tears began to well in Mara's eyes. She turned to face the window. "It means," she said, her voice quavering, "that Dr. Hoo has been kidnapped."

# THE THIRD NIGHT

Fiercer than lava,
Stronger than stone,
Harder than iron,
Brighter than bone,
Sharper than teeth,
Deeper than fear —
Answer this, friend,
And see it appear.


— an ancient gathool riddle

# 27

"It doesn't make sense," Zak said. "Who could've kidnapped Dr. Hoo?"

Mara hesitated. She glanced nervously at Thora. "The *gathool* took him," she said. "I'm afraid he's being held by the trolls now."

The room was silent for a moment. Then Thora leaped to her feet. Her face was red and her fists were clenched. "Say it," she said. "Go ahead, say it! We're all thinking it. The doctor disappeared because my brother took him. That's why his pocket knife is here. Bryce carved 'croatoan' into the wall with his knife, then left it here!"

Mara unfolded her arms and stuck her hands in

the pockets of her long coat. "I don't know for sure," she said. "But, yes, it looks that way."

Thora covered her face with her hands and stood weeping in the middle of the room. Louise ran over to her and wrapped her arms around Thora's waist.

Zak's heart sank as he stared at Thora. She had been so brave. Just two nights ago, she had helped save them all from two giant trolls. But now, Thora looked weak and small. *I guess that's normal,* Zak thought. *After all, the world is basically coming to an end.*

"Maybe Bryce was taken too," Pablo said quietly. "Maybe he tried to help Dr. Hoo, but couldn't. Maybe he left his pocket knife here as a sign." Pablo looked back at Thora, who peered at him through the damp strands of her hair. "To let you know where they took him," he added.

Thora sniffed. She wiped the tears from her cheeks. "You think so?" she said.

"Sure," said Pablo. "But I still don't get what that word means." He pointed at the word *croatoan*, carved deeply into the wood.

Zak crossed his arms. "It doesn't matter what the word means," he said. "What matters is they're both gone, just like my parents. And we have to go find them."

Mara shook her head. "It's too dangerous," she said.

"What do you mean?" Zak asked.

"It's likely that the trolls are trying to lure you underground to their realm," Mara said. "It's almost certainly a trap."

"We've defeated the trolls before," argued Zak. "Twice, in fact. The doctor showed us how."

Thora tucked her hair behind her ears. "I agree with Zak," she said. "The doctor saved us. Now we have to save him."

Mara sighed. She looked over at the wooden table near the center of the room. Dr. Hoo's library was crammed with hundreds of books. "I gave those books on the top of the table to Dr. Hoo," she said.

Mara walked over, selected one book, and flipped through its pages. She stopped at a particular page and opened the book toward the others. "Listen to this," she said, reading aloud: "An ancient prophecy among the *gathool* has warned them for centuries of a deadly 'band of light' that could destroy their species. But the *gathool* vocabulary is small; their mouths are limited in the sounds they can make. So few words must stand for many things. 'Band' can also mean 'ring' or 'circle.' 'Light' can also stand for 'gold,' 'shining,' or 'pain.'"

Thora nodded. "That's what the doctor read to us the other night," she said. "He said it meant that sunlight could defeat the trolls."

"It turns them to stone," added Pablo.

"It means something else, too," said Mara. "The *gathool* can only be defeated by a 'band of light.' That does refer to the sun, but also means a band of companions."

"Like . . . a rock band?" asked Zak.

Mara shot Zak a confused look. "What? No, of course not," she said.

Zak's face turned red. "Then what do you mean?" he asked defensively.

"A band of companions, or friends," Mara said. "A

band of warriors. Warriors whose brilliant light can defeat the trolls, just like sunlight.

*Just like when Pablo, Louise, Thora, and I had radiated light as we battled,* Zak thought.

"Dr. Hoo told me that you were chosen for this fight," said Mara. "He's spoken of you all for many years."

"But how?" asked Pablo. "He never met us before last night."

"I'm not sure," Mara said. "But Dr. Hoo was convinced that Zion Falls was going to be the next battleground between the forces of darkness and the forces of light. He knew that the *gathool* would use places in this town as their entry points to the surface."

"Like the old well on the Nye farm," said Pablo.

"And the pit under the silo," said Thora.

Pablo stood. "We have to get to that old well," he said. "If the trolls have taken Bryce and the doctor underground, then that's how they'd get back to their world."

"What makes you so sure?" asked Zak.

Pablo shook his head. "I don't know," he said. "It just . . . feels right."

Zak stared at Pablo. He glimpsed a weird light in Pablo's eyes. Starlight. He had seen it before — and each time, it felt like the two of them were connected.

Zak nodded confidently. "Yeah," he said. "I think you're right."

"Then it's settled," said Thora. "How far is the well from here?"

Mara stepped forward. "No," she said firmly. Everyone turned to look at her. "You aren't going to the well."

"What are you talking about?" Zak snapped. "That's the only way underground."

"No," repeated Mara. "It's not. There is a way to the troll kingdom that is much closer."

Mara took a step toward the wall. She raised her finger, pointing at the word etched into its surface. "*Croatoan*," she said, "is a *gathool* word that means 'bridge to the underworld'."

Puzzled faces stared back at Mara. She opened her hands to take in all of the tower. "The *gathool* have marked this tower as a gateway to the their kingdom," she explained. "And we're going to use it to enter their world."

# 28

With each step downward, Bryce Gamble found it harder to breathe. He and the doctor were marching deeper and deeper into the endless tunnels below the earth. The air was thick and hot, and felt heavy like it did before a summer storm in Zion Falls.

Bryce wasn't sure how he had gotten here. Only darkness surrounded him. Darkness and smoke.

*Hrooooom . . . hroom . . .*

A drum-like beat sounded from below. Bryce's shuffling feet marched along to the rhythm of the sound as he walked through the rocky tunnel. He and the doctor were being pulled farther below the surface by some powerful unseen force.

Bryce could see the shadowy outlines of others marching with them. Seven or eight others, all moving forward in complete silence. Some of the figures looked familiar to Bryce, but he couldn't remember their faces or their names.

Bryce only remembered the doctor. He could see him clearly now, despite the darkness. And he could see the golden chains around all of their wrists. Bryce was a prisoner. So was the doctor. But why?

Bryce felt like he was no longer in control of his actions. Some power had moved him like a puppet without strings. The power had forced him to enter the doctor's house and confront the doctor. To kidnap him.

*But did I actually kidnap him?* Bryce thought. *After all, my hands are chained, too. What's going on?*

The drum pounded, and his feet obeyed. They all marched mindlessly along their hot, horrible journey. But who — or what — was beating that drum?

And where was Thora?

# 29

In Dr. Hoo's library, something strange was happening. The entire library shook. The four large windows of the octagonal room went black. A low hum vibrated through the air.

Thora fell to the floor. She sat down hard in the middle of the doctor's library, the room shaking around her. *Why do I feel so dizzy?* she thought. *Is this some evil trick of the* gathool?

Louise collapsed into Thora's lap. The little girl stared up at her with wide and fearful eyes. "What's happening?" Louise pleaded, but Thora could barely hear her.

Thora glanced around for Pablo. She saw him on

the nearby couch. He was trying to stand up, but he kept falling back onto the cushions.

Zak was still on his feet, but he jerked and wobbled like a puppet. He bent his knees and held his arms out for balance. Slowly, as if he were moving underwater, he trudged toward the library door.

"No!" screamed Mara. "Don't —"

Zak opened the door. A burst of red light and sound threw him backward into the room. A grinding roar shuddered through the building. Wind rushed through the door, blowing books off shelves, and stirring up cyclones of dust.

Thora shielded her face. She saw flashes of crimson light rushing past the library entrance as if they were on a merry-go-round.

"We're turning," Thora cried. "The building is turning!"

Mara staggered over to the door and slammed it shut. The wind stopped and the grinding sound quieted. She hurried over to Zak and kneeled, putting a hand on his shoulder. "Are you all right?" she asked.

"What's going on?" Zak said. "What's out there!?"

"The word on the wall — *croatoan*," Mara began. "The *gathool* warriors use the word whenever they need to leave a message behind for their comrades. It lets others know how to return home."

Pablo stood up from the couch. "Then we need to get there," he said.

Mara nodded. "But there is only one way to travel. By using ancient *gathool* technology. By using a *croatoan*."

*Technology?* Thora wondered. Then she remembered. In their most recent battle against the trolls, the creatures had been approaching the surface inside a weird tower-like vessel. It had risen through layers of rock and lava like a rocket made of stone.

"The tower is descending!" Thora exclaimed.

"Yes," said Mara. "I don't know how or why, but it must have something to do with the power inside each of you. The doctor always said you four are linked together."

"What do you mean?" Thora asked.

"Dr. Hoo said that his tower would react to your desires when the time came," Mara explained. "I didn't realize before now that Dr. Hoo's tower is a vessel that will take us into the heart of the *gathool* world."

Zak propped himself up on the floor. "So," he said, "this house is taking us to the trolls' realm?"

Mara smiled at him. "Your unified desire to save the doctor, and your friends and family, must have activated the tower gateway, or *croatoan*," she said. "Otherwise, it never would have moved."

Zak shook his head. "That's crazy," he said. "How can thoughts move an object? It's just not realistic."

"But Zak," said Thora, "think about what we've seen lately. The silo, the trolls, how we all . . . changed. Into warriors."

Zak hesitated. "I guess," he said. "I just figured we'd climb down some well, scare a few of the trolls, and then drag the doctor's butt back up here. Or . . . up there." He glanced up at the library's ceiling. "Uh, where exactly are we?"

Mara walked to a book sitting on a wooden stand in the center of the room. "I'm not sure," she replied. She flipped to the back of the book, reading the doctor's notes aloud. "'Reaching the entrance to the trolls' realm likely involves traveling through solid rock, of course, but also some kind of barrier. Something like a different dimension.'"

Zak rolled his eyes. "Every time you answer a question," he said, "you make even less sense."

"Maybe it's like a wormhole," suggested Pablo.

Everyone stared blankly at Pablo.

"You know," Pablo continued, "like, a single point that allows you to travel immediately across vast distances."

Thora arched an eyebrow and grinned. "Where did you hear about that?" she asked.

Pablo smirked. "My dad and I used to watch a lot of *Star Trek* reruns," he said. "In one episode, Captain Picard said that wormholes were like secret passages between different parts of the universe." He trailed off, suddenly embarrassed.

Thora smiled at Pablo. "I used to watch *Star Trek* too," she said warmly. Pablo smiled.

"Actually," Mara said, "that's not very different from how the doctor explained it to me."

Louise was still lying next to Thora with her head in Thora's lap. "So . . . are we flying up?" Louise asked. "Or going down?"

Thora could tell Louise was scared and trying to hide it. "I don't know, Louise," Thora said. "But at least we're all together. Remember how you helped me back at the silo?"

"Sort of," said Louise. "I helped you lift that jar."

"Exactly," Thora said. "Your power of balance helped us win that fight."

Louise sat up, smiling. "Yeah! I helped us win!" she repeated. "Cool!"

Zak stood up, then he took a few steps and turned to face Thora. "So where's that golden jar now?" he asked her.

Thora rolled her eyes. "It's not like I can pull it out of my pocket," she said.

"So where is it?" Zak repeated.

Pablo walked up to Zak. "Where's that bear I saw?" he challenged. "You know, Ursa Major."

"Oh yeah, the bear!" said Louise. She let out a little roar and started giggling.

Zak looked down at his chest and his arms. "Let's find out," he said. He closed his eyes tightly and took a few deep breaths. His face started to turn red as he tensed all his muscles.

Thora grinned. "What exactly are you trying to do?" she asked.

Zak opened his eyes and let out a breath. "I'm focusing, okay?" he said. "I thought maybe if I concentrated —"

"What?" interrupted Pablo. "You'd turn into a bear?"

Thora laughed.

Zak smirked. "Got any better ideas, Mr. Know-It-All?" he asked.

Pablo put his hand on Zak's shoulder. "Sorry," Pablo said. "But I just don't think it works that way."

"I think our powers work whenever we really need them," Thora suggested. "But that's just a guess."

Zak walked over to the couch and plopped down. "Great," he said. "What good are superpowers if you can't use them when you want to?"

Thora squinted hard at Zak's hands. She saw that his fingers were glowing. A silver radiance was creeping up Zak's wrists and arms.

"Zak!" cried Thora.

Zak looked at her. "What, weirdo?"

"Zak!" said Louise.

"What is your problem?" Zak asked.

"Look at your hands!" Thora said.

Thora watched Zak look at his hands. His eyes went wide. A smile slowly crept up to the corners of his mouth. "It's happening!" he said.

"Thora!" cried Louise. "Look at me!" She stood. She seemed as tall as Mara now. Her hair was longer, and it flickered back and forth as if an invisible wind ran through it.

"Why is this happening now?" asked Thora.

Mara raised her hand, motioning for everyone to be quiet. They all listened. The faint grinding sound was gone. The library room had stopped moving. The windows, which had been dark rectangles before, now let in a faint reddish light from beyond. The light danced around them like flames.

One of the windows suddenly lit up with a bright red blaze. The glass shattered and went flying across the room.

Something in the window hissed at them. Louise screamed.

"*Agna gathool*," cried Mara. "Fire trolls!"

# 30

The troll known as Uzhk stopped at the mouth of a new tunnel that sloped downward at a steep angle. Uzhk peered in and stared at the far end. He made a strange sound in his throat that a human may have thought sounded like a gulp.

This was the passageway that Uzhk had been seeking ever since he left the human farm far above him. The sight of the great tower rising up from within the abandoned silo had spurred him to come this way.

Uzhk had seen similar vessels invading the surface before. Centuries ago, they had pierced through openings around the early American colonies. They had attacked armies on horseback in the far fields of Mongolia. The great vessels had soared upward into the Bermuda islands. Each time, they were defeated by the *prak tara* — the children of the stars.

But Uzhk had learned a lesson from those battles. The *gathool*, his evil brethren, never attacked in just one place. More *gathool* warships, like the one beneath the silo, would be launched, and they would be carrying larger and deadlier warriors. He hoped he could reach the heart of the attacks, the ones who were sending the dark towers into the world of humans. If he could somehow stop them from attacking the surface . . .

Uzhk stared hard at the far end of the tunnel. Golden light gleamed steadily at the exit. It was the barrier to the *gathool* kingdom, a wall of golden light. It was merely a tiny section of a powerful, glowing sphere that lay buried in the Earth's mantle. The sphere's wall was thin, Uzhk knew, thinner than a finger on his friend Mara's hand. "Thin as a piece of paper," Dr. Hoo had told him. But the golden light was deadly to all trolls, the evil *gathool* and Uzhk's *drakhool* brethren alike.

It had been many years since Uzhk had come this way, when he first left the kingdom of darkness for the world of light. The world of humans. Back then, he had help.

This time, he would have to pass through the wall by himself.

On the other side of the deadly wall were the two beings he had to find. One was a human. The other was the wearer of the Lava Crown, the general of the *gathool* army, the creature who had ordered the *gathool* invasion.

Uzhk struck his chest with his massive hands and bellowed out a war cry. He lowered his head and ran down the tunnel.

The steep angle added to his momentum. Faster and faster he ran. The golden rays burned into his rocky flesh. His eyes blazed with pain. He feared they would sizzle in their sockets and pop out of his skull. But he kept running.

Then, suddenly, the giant figure passed into the golden curtain of light.

# 31

Two unearthly beings skittered through the broken library window. Their burning breaths moved the curtains by the window, causing the fabric to catch fire as the creatures passed by.

Pablo thought the creatures looked like upright lizards. They had sharp claws, several eyes, and thick scales. Their skin glowed orange-red like coals beneath a smoldering campfire.

*How many different kinds of trolls are there?!* he wondered. *These ones look like ferocious dinosaur-spiders.*

*Pablo,* a voice whispered in Pablo's mind. The voice was warm and cozy, like a fireplace on a winter morning.

*Pablo . . . you know nothing . . . you can't stop us.*

"What?" Pablo yelled.

The monstrous trolls let out a terrifying collective hiss that each of the humans heard as a different sound. To Louise, the hiss sounded like her pet rabbit screaming. Zak heard the screech of tires as his parents cried out in pain. Thora heard her brother calling out for her help. Mara heard the doctor's voice calling her foolish for letting the children enter the realm of the trolls.

The hiss tore through Pablo's mind like a hot knife. To him, the voice sounded like Thora, but it was far crueler than she'd ever been. "You stupid nerd," the voice howled. "It's your fault we're going to die here!"

The hiss stopped as a thunderous roar broke out beside him. The nimble trolls lurched back in surprise when a colossal silver bear reared up and roared, baring its gleaming fangs. Then the bear charged forward and swiped its massive paws at the trolls.

Pablo tried to warn Zak that the trolls might burn him, but the shout got caught in his throat. Somehow,

his hand was once again grasping a sword, just as it had back at the silo.

Pablo smiled and dashed forward to fight alongside his friend, the marauding bear. The huge grizzly and his warrior companion stood before the fire trolls, attacking them with claws and blades and teeth.

Suddenly, a troll hissed. Below its burning eyes, a mouth filled with jagged teeth opened wide. A jet of flame spurted from the troll's throat. "Look out!" shouted Pablo as he shoved the big bear to the side.

The fireball shot between him and Zak and burst into a bookshelf, turning it into a pile of smoldering ashes. Another stream of fire swooshed from the troll's jaws and missed Louise's long hair by mere inches. She ducked and jumped to the side, flying past Thora. She was hovering several feet above the floor!

Thora didn't have time to marvel at this new demonstration of the younger girl's powers. Instead, she turned her attention to the fire trolls. They moved carefully and quickly, barely making a sound — except when they belched searing flames. Bookshelves, furniture, and scientific artifacts were already wreathed in fire. The library's ceiling had filled with thick, acrid puffs of smoke.

Mara had emerged from behind the bookcase. She was spraying a fire extinguisher on the table of Dr. Hoo's books. Thora ran to her and helped pat out flames that danced along the books' covers and spines.

Zak roared again and swung his paw at the fire trolls. Finally, he connected with one of the beasts and knocked the troll on its side. Searing pain ran up Zak's bear-arm all the way to his shoulder. His skin and fur burned.

Zak howled so loudly that the air quivered like heat rippling off a hot road. The reverberation caused the fallen troll's scales to crack and break. Hot magma oozed from the troll's husk. It let out a final hiss and died.

Pablo swung his sword at the second troll, managing to slice off one of its limbs. When the troll opened its mouth and hissed, Pablo knew what was coming. He instinctively raised his left arm to protect himself — and a silver shield appeared. Its gleaming surface deflected the troll's flames and sent the fire back in the beast's face.

However, the troll kept moving forward. Then another troll crawled through the window and joined the fight.

*Zak and I are barely slowing them down,* thought Pablo. *The trolls might not kill us, but the fire will.*

Pablo turned to look for Thora. He saw her standing near the book table. Their eyes met. Pablo saw a sparkle in Thora's eyes. As if she could hear his thoughts, Thora gave Pablo a quick nod.

Suddenly, a rushing breeze passed through the room as pages from the books were lifted up in a whirlwind. The pages circled Thora like a cyclone of paper. She grew taller as the flying pages clung to her skin and transformed into a silver gown made of flowing fabric. Ornate armor grew around her torso. A gleaming helmet graced the top of her head. The jar from the previous battle was not in sight, but Pablo knew that didn't matter. Thora was ready for battle.

Thora aimed her arms at one of the fire trolls. A burst of wind sent the creature flying out the window.

Just then, Zak cried out in pain. Another troll had wrapped its long tongue around Zak's bear-feet, tripping him to the ground. His furry skin sizzled where the tongue was latched onto his legs.

Pablo moved toward his friend and repeatedly hacked at the tongue with his sword. Another troll maneuvered itself behind Pablo. With his back to his enemy, he and Zak were left unprotected.

The troll's jaws opened. It began coughing up a glob of searing flame.Then the entire room tilted toward the broken window. The trolls slid backward as the jet of flame erupted from the troll's roaring mouth.

Since the troll had been knocked off-balance, the fire flew wide of its aim, narrowly missing Zak and Pablo.

*How?* thought Pablo. He looked back to see Louise floating above the floor, smiling. She looked like a beautiful teenage girl wearing clothes from an ancient era. Her eyes were closed, but she was moving her hands up and down. It seemed as if she were causing the floor to shift like the deck of a ship in water.

A wide wave of silver water slammed against the trolls in the form of a huge tidal wave. Thora aimed her arms at the trolls and a gust of wind struck the water, directing waves past Zak and Pablo and toward the hideous slugs. Higher and higher the water rose within the library. Waves circled the room like a whirlpool.

The trolls were hurled through the glass and out the window in a gust of bright foam.

Then the water began to recede. It leaked out the walls, the door frame, and through cracks in the floorboards. Louise slowly settled back onto the floor, standing on her own feet again. She breathed a sigh of relief.

Pablo stood, shaking his head, his Roman-style armor and weapons gone. Then he saw Zak holding his legs in pain, buckled over on the floor.

"Are you okay?" Pablo asked, rushing toward him.

Zak shook his head. "I don't know," he said through clenched teeth. His skin was red and blistered where the troll's tongue had grabbed him. Blood seeped from the gashes.

Thora and Mara knelt next to him. "Maybe there's a first aid kit somewhere in here," Mara suggested.

"No," said Thora calmly. "Let me." She reached out and gently touched Zak's ankles. He started to pull away in pain. "Hold still," she said, smiling. Her hand closed over his burns as she looked into Zak's eyes. Thora's hand began to glow with a golden radiance.

"Ahh!" Zak cried out.

"Help me," Thora said, looking first at Pablo, then at Louise. The two moved closer to Thora and placed their own hands on top of hers. The golden light from her hand grew instantly.

It wrapped around Zak's ankles and began to enclose all of their hands. Soon, all four friends were encased in a sphere of light. The golden glow turned to a bright silver.

*Starlight,* thought Pablo. Suddenly, a blinding flash burst through the room.

"My leg!" cried Zak. He blinked tightly. As he opened his eyes, he held his leg up to see. His flesh was no longer red or burned. It was healed.

"Wow!" Zak said. Then he stared at Thora. "How'd you know how to do that?"

Thora shrugged and smiled. "Dunno, she said. "Instinct, I guess."

Zak shook his head in disbelief. "I never felt anything like that before."

Pablo nodded. He flexed his fingers. He noticed his hand felt empty and naked without a sword in it. The thirst for battle was growing inside of him, even though the trolls were gone.

Pablo looked over at Mara. "Did you hear their voices?" he asked. "When they first attacked? Like, in your head?"

"We are in the *gathool's* world now," Mara said. "Their powers are stronger here."

"Do you think they'll attack again?" Pablo asked.

"I don't know," said Mara. "But we have to move. The trolls know we're here."

Zak smirked. "You think?" he said. "The giant fire-dinosaur-spider troll attack made that pretty obvious."

Louise stood. "The fire's out," she said. They

glanced around at the charred remains of the library. Only one book had survived the flames. Mara cradled *The Book of Stars* in her arms.

Thora gazed out the windows. "There are fires burning everywhere in this world," she said.

Pablo wasn't surprised. He was sure they'd see much more fire — and fighting — before the day was over. They were in the trolls' world now.

"Well, we might as well do what we came here for," Zak said. "Let's go save the doctor."

# 32

Dr. Hoo shuffled along with the other humans.

*Hroom . . . hroom . . .*

His movements weren't controlled by the powerful drumbeat like the others were. He knew exactly where the pull of the *gathool* was taking them. He had been there many times before. But it was important that the other humans thought he was the *gathool's* prisoner, just like they were.

Suddenly, the marching stopped. Bryce Gamble, Thora's brother, was next to him.

Farther back was Louise's father, Mr. Tooker, followed by Zak's parents, the Fishers.

They had all reached the entrance to the heart of

the *gathool* kingdom. Their escort of powerful troll warriors stepped aside and pulled open the massive stone doors. The humans gasped and blinked at the countless crimson fires illuminating the jagged tunnel.

The entrance opened into a vast cavern a thousand times greater than any coliseum or stadium. Dr. Hoo saw Bryce gaze at it in awe. *This is his first time here,* Dr. Hoo thought. *He probably feels like an insect that's been plopped into the center of the old quarry outside Zion Falls. I know I did the first time I saw it.*

As the travelers moved forward, the tunnel emerged into a rocky bridge. The bridge led toward a gigantic mesa thrusting upward in the center. They had entered a volcano's magma chamber. The doctor glanced down the side of the bridge. Churning molten lava surrounded the mesa. Waves of lava rose and fell, crashing into each other in immense torrents of thundering flame. It was the source of the fiery light that illuminated the vast chamber.

The distant, curving walls were as tall as mountains. Lights and shadows played across their rocky surfaces. The ceiling of the coliseum was draped in shadows.

*HROOM . . . HROOM . . .*

The pulsing beat grew louder.

The humans marched involuntarily across the narrow causeway, heading for the mesa's heart. Fear was written all over their faces, but they could not resist the beat of the drum.

Something glowed at the center of the raised rock, but it was still too far for anyone to see. The doctor knew they were close to its source, which gave it even more power.

*Ooloom,* a voice whispered inside the doctor's head. *Bow to Ooloom.*

The humans looked at each other with confused glances. They all seemed to be asking themselves, "Did the others hear it?"

Then the whisper came again. *All hail Ooloom,* it said. *The wearer of the Lava Crown.*

Onward they marched, wide-eyed and fearful. Walls of heat rose upward from the vast sea and shimmered past them. Several times the doctor thought Bryce might faint, but the relentless drum pulled him forward anyway.

*Hroom . . . Ooloom . . .*

Unlike Dr. Hoo, the other humans didn't know that the drumming sound was in their heads. It was a psychic whisper that the wearer of the Lava Crown sent into their minds, compelling them to come to him. The closer they were, the stronger his influence on them would be. A cold chill slid across the back of Dr. Hoo's neck. He felt the Lava Crown's influence beginning to affect him as well.

As they neared the center of the mesa, they all saw the glowing object at the center. A brilliant statue, with veins pulsing like lava, sat atop the great mesa. The humans all gasped and trembled. Atop its head rested a glowing ring of magma fashioned in the shape of a crown. Even the sight made Dr. Hoo shrink back. Its power was immense. Vast.

Dr. Hoo saw Bryce close his eyes as the fear burned within him. All the humans were starting to feel an overpowering sense of fear and dread. *It's fortunate the effect is half as strong for me,* Dr. Hoo thought. *Otherwise, I'd be powerless right now — just like them.*

A commotion behind Dr. Hoo distracted him from his thoughts. A troll was racing toward the center of the mesa.

Other trolls tried to stop the figure, but it was relentless. It stormed forward, crushing and throwing aside everything in its path. The frantic creature looked as if it were carved from rock, with huge slabs for arms.

The troll kept pushing forward until it reached the front of the line — and the doctor. Dr. Hoo looked up into the creature's face and frowned. "Uzhk!" he said. "What are you doing here?!"

The troll uttered rough, rasping sounds. "We are brothers," Uzhk said in his own language. He lifted Dr. Hoo's shirt, and pointed at the third arm protruding from his chest.

The crowd of humans gasped at the strange sight. "We are brothers by blood and magma, sons of one mother," Uzhk said. "Our voices speak the same tongue. Together, we can stop this war! Unite with me!"

The doctor stared sadly at the friendly monster.

He shook his head back and forth slowly. "I cannot," Dr. Hoo said.

"But the *prak tara* —" said Uzhk.

The doctor raised his arms — all three of them — above his head and tensed his muscles. A flash of intense red light burst from his hands. Uzhk was hurled backward across the mesa. He crashed headlong onto the ground near the edge of a cliff, his face facing downward at the ocean of lava beneath them.

"We are . . . brothers," moaned the troll. Several cracks ran through his rocky figure. Molten lava seeped out from the wounds.

"We were brothers," the doctor said coldly. He gestured at his third arm. "But, as the saying goes, you've forced my hand."

Uzhk's rocky face turned dark. "Brother," he croaked. "Please don't turn your back on the *drakhool*. On the humans. On me."

Dr. Hoo turned to the other humans, ignoring Uzhk. He snapped his fingers. Instantly, the golden chains that were latched around his wrists vanished.

"Forward!" Dr. Hoo ordered the chained humans. "March . . . or die."

The doctor watched Bryce struggle against his bonds. The boy whimpered in pain as the gold seared his flesh whenever he moved.

"Forward!" Dr. Hoo repeated.

Suddenly, with a rumble that threw the humans off their feet, the glowing statue rose from its seated position. It stood tall before them, pulsing with dark energy.

It grew higher and higher, like a hill of stone. And the bright crown on top grew larger with it. The creature's red eyes were made of molten lava. Lava also shone brightly in its mouth. Its massive chest heaved in and out. With each long, mighty throb, the drumbeat sounded in the humans' ears. Eerie words joined the rhythm. *Ooloom. Ooloom. Ooloom.*

Dr. Hoo knelt and bowed his head. Bryce glanced at the doctor's third arm. "Who — what — are you?" Bryce sputtered.

For a moment, Dr. Hoo looked hurt. But before he or Bryce could say anything more, the crowned

giant slowly turned its gaze toward Bryce. The roar of
scraping rocks filled the chamber. Then an ugly voice
whispered into their minds.

He is. My servant, it said. His task. Was to bring.
You all. To me.

A spark of fire shot upward from the Lava Crown.
Bryce and the other humans cried out in pain and fell,
unconscious, to the rocky floor.

The living rock wearing the crown spoke directly
into Dr. Hoo's mind. You have. Done well, it said.
Deceiver.

Dr. Hoo said nothing.

# 33

The tunnel angled sharply downward. Thora and the others carefully traveled over stony ledges and rough ridges. The rocky floor of the tunnel felt hot beneath Thora's feet as she walked. The walls were warm against her palms when she leaned on them for support.

"I'm surprised we haven't seen more trolls so far," Thora said.

Zak grunted. "I'm not," he said. "They're probably just waiting for us to come to them."

In the tunnel's dim light, Mara held *The Book of Stars* close to her face, trying to make out the ancient scrawls traced on the book's final pages. "If

I'm reading this map correctly," she said in a hushed voice, "then we're almost there."

Thora knew they were approaching their goal without having to read a map. She could sense the looming threat, and they were starting to respond physically. Louise's voice had changed, seeming more mature. The younger girl holding Thora's hand was growing taller, too. Pablo's silhouette, up ahead, now included a helmet and weapons. Thora felt a new weight grow upon her shoulders as her armor started to appear once again.

"How's your arm doing, Zak?" Thora asked. The boy behind her merely growled. She turned, and saw that Zak had the head and arms of a bear.

"That's a good look for you," Thora teased. A gruff noise that sounded vaguely like a laugh came from Zak's throat.

Suddenly, Thora heard a familiar voice echo in her mind.

*Thora . . . help me . . .*

Thora had heard Bryce's voice in her head once before — just outside the doctor's house. Bryce had whispered to her, asking her for help. She didn't know it was him at the time. Back then, Bryce's voice had sounded strained and twisted — not like him at all. This time was different. He sounded like himself now.

Thora knew he was in danger. She knew he needed her help. "Bryce is here!" she said. She raced down the sloping tunnel toward the exit. The others quickly followed.

Soon, they plunged out of the darkness and into a vast, fiery chamber. Waves of burning magma thundered and rolled on every side. Thora didn't stop. She kept running along the bridge.

*Please . . . help me . . . Thora . . .*

"Bryce!" Thora yelled. "Where are you?!"

"Thora, stop!" cried Mara.

Hideous creatures stood on both sides of Thora's path, but they didn't move to stop her. Their eyes were turned toward the center of the massive mesa.

*That's where Bryce is,* Thora thought. *I will save you this time, big bro.*

The others ran hard, trying to catch up with her. As Thora neared the center of the mesa, she saw a gigantic statue with a flaming crown atop its head. At the statue's feet was a group of humans lying on their sides. All of them had golden chains around their hands and legs. Nearest to her lay Bryce, his eyes barely open.

"Bryce!" screamed Thora. She ran up and kneeled next to her brother.

"Bryce," she whispered. "Are you all right?"

Bryce's pale face gazed up at her. "Thora?" he asked uncertainly.

Thora felt the helmet on her head. Her transformation was complete. *I guess I look pretty different to Bryce like this,* she thought. "Yes, it's me," she said.

Bryce lifted a hand toward her strange armor. With his finger, he traced an engraving of swirling stars that decorated her armor. He smiled weakly. "Wow," he said.

Thora smiled. "Everything's going to be all right, big bro," she said.

Bryce began to shiver. "I . . . I did this," he said. "I brought us all here. Into this trap. I'm . . . I'm so sorry."

*Ooloom.* A voice pounded in Thora's ears. Thora looked up and gasped as the statue shifted toward her. She felt its burning eyes, bright as comets, reach deep inside her core. Just then, the others caught up to Thora. They stood behind her, uncertain of what to do.

Then, out from behind the monstrous troll's leg, stepped a familiar figure. "Doctor!" shouted Mara.

Dr. Hoo now stood several paces away from where Bryce lay. He walked toward the young warriors, confusion and surprise covering their faces.

"Doc!" Zak said. "We're here to rescue you!" Zak was now a bear, and his voice came out gruff and deep.

The doctor recognized him. He smiled wide. Then he raised his three arms upward. Instantly, the mesa exploded in scarlet brilliance. Everyone fell to the ground.

Thora cried out in pain. She looked up at the doctor in horror. "What are you . . . doing?" she whimpered.

*Ooloom.* The giant troll gazed down at the fallen humans. A thunderous voice bellowed throughout the entire chamber. "You have. Done well," the giant troll said. It looked at Dr. Hoo, adding, "My servant."

The doctor bowed his head. All three of his hands were open and held out toward the giant creature.

The young warriors' eyes all went wide. "No!" Zak growled. "It's not possible! You can't be one of them!"

A hiss reverberated throughout the vast chamber, growing louder and louder. It seemed to circle them like an evil wind. Thora heard more voices join in the sinister sound. The hissing grew louder.

"Uzhk!" Mara cried. She pointed toward the edge of the mesa where it dropped off into the lava sea. A strange-looking troll lay there, collapsed.

Then Thora saw more figures just beyond the collapsed troll. The entire mesa was ringed in a curtain of dark shadows. She saw then that it was a multitude of trolls. Monstrous, many-headed, many-handed beings all marched toward the Lava Crown. The circle of warriors grew tighter as they surrounded the powerless humans. The hiss they cried out was deafening.

The giant nodded his colossal head, his crown

sputtering with flames. He spoke to his subjects. "*Prak tara marith yoo,*" the giant rumbled. The giant troll looked at the young heroes, then at the doctor. "The children of the stars must die."

The doctor nodded. He raised his arms once again. A golden light appeared above their heads, spinning like a disc. The light separated into distinct rings, forming a long, golden chain.

Slowly, the chain floated down toward the young heroes and landed on the ground with a thud. Before they could react, the shackles connected around their hands and their feet, chaining them.

The army of a million trolls marched forward. The ring grew tighter. Thora saw *The Book of Stars* lying face down on the ground where Mara had dropped it.

Thora remembered the words the doctor had read to them from it, that first night in his house. The ancient prophecies talked about a band of gold that would defeat the trolls. These shackles were bands of gold.

*The doctor lied to us,* Thora thought. *He tricked all of us.*

Suddenly Zak growled. "Mom, Dad!" he yelled. He lurched forward, but the chain sizzled around his limbs and brought him crashing painfully to the ground. He howled in pain.

Thora saw the Fishers among the crowd of human prisoners lying on the ground. All of them were unconscious, but breathing.

*Bands of gold,* Thora thought, noticing their chains. *The doctor captured us all with bands of gold.*

Zak lay on his side, racked with pain. He strained to reach his arm out toward his parents. "I have to . . . help them," he whimpered. The chains sizzled around his limbs.

Hate burned inside Thora. She glared at the doctor, watching him bow his head as he kneeled toward the crowned troll.

"You traitor!" Thora yelled.

# 34

Dr. Hoo rose into the air over the heads of the young humans, red waves of light emanating from him. Bryce watched the bottoms of the doctor's shoes recede as he rose higher and higher into the air. Soon, the doctor was face to face with the fiery giant.

As the giant's gaze turned toward Dr. Hoo and away from the humans, Bryce felt momentary relief. He could breathe again without pain.

But the troll army's feet still shook the ground as the trolls continued to close the circle around the humans.

Another hot gust of wind blew across the mesa as the giant looked at the hovering doctor.

"You have. Brought them," the creature growled. "For me."

"Yes, Ooloom," Dr. Hoo said. "As a gift for you."

*Ooloom,* Bryce thought. The name made him shiver despite the heat.

"A sacrifice," Ooloom bellowed. "To me."

"Just as you deserve," Dr. Hoo said. "Ooloom, Wearer of the Lava Crown."

Bryce looked at his sister. He could tell Thora's pain had also lessened, but her face was still twisted in agony. She was staring at the golden shackles around their limbs with disgust. She caught Bryce's gaze and whispered, "He betrayed us all. He made a deal with that . . . monster."

Bryce clenched his teeth. *He did this,* he thought. *The doctor betrayed my sister.*

Furious, Bryce strained against his chains, trying to break them. Instead, it just pulled the chains taut against all four heroes. They let out a collective scream as the golden shackles seared into their skin.

Ooloom laughed, lava spitting out from his rocky lips. "There is. No escape," he growled.

Bryce glanced at Dr. Hoo. There was a pained look on the doctor's face. *Wait,* the doctor whispered into Bryce's mind. *Wait.*

Bryce's eyes went wide. *What does he mean?* Bryce thought. He turned to see Thora looking at him with wide eyes. *She heard it too.*

Ooloom turned his gaze back to the doctor. His voice rumbled throughout the fiery cavern. "You too. Must bow. To Ooloom."

The doctor smiled widely and spread his three arms out in a gesture of peace and submission. "I have always obeyed those who are more powerful than me," Dr. Hoo said.

Ooloom's laugh sounded like gravel and roaring fire. "You are. Very weak," he said.

"I have never been as strong as you, Ooloom," Dr. Hoo said. "I am only half-troll, unlike you. But I take comfort in the power of my ancestors."

"Words. Words," replied the giant. "You bore. Ooloom."

"Words can be power," Dr. Hoo said calmly. "The *gathool* have always respected power, am I correct?"

Ooloom stiffened. "Yes," he said reluctantly. "It is. Our way."

The doctor closed his eyes and bowed his head. He began chanting a rhyme:

*"Fiercer than lava,*

*Stronger than stone,*

*Harder than iron,*

*Brighter than bone.*

*Sharper than teeth*

*Deeper than fear —*

*Answer this, friend,*

*And see it appear."*

Dr. Hoo nodded almost imperceptibly at Bryce. Then he turned to face Ooloom. "The ancient riddle," Dr. Hoo said, "reminds us of the greatest power of all. What is fiercer than lava? What is deeper and stronger than fear?"

The giant began to sway back and forth. The Lava Crown glowed an angry red. "Silence!" he growled.

"Friend," Thora whispered to Bryce. "The answer is friend."

*Answer this, friend, and see it appear,* Bryce

repeated in his mind. *Friend. By speaking the word 'friend', you identify yourself as one.*

Bryce nodded at Thora. "He's distracted," he said. "Now's our chance."

Thora nodded. She grabbed Bryce's hand and held it tightly. The chains burned her, but she silently strained against them and reached for Pablo's foot. "Pablo," she whispered. "Grab on to Louise."

Pablo nodded. He quietly shifted his body and reached over to Louise.

"The band of gold," whispered Thora. "Companions. Friends. We have to close the circle."

Bryce felt another hand touch his shoulder. He looked over and saw Louise was leaning across the ground, reaching for him. The band of gold was almost complete.

The trolls moved closer. The rhythmic beating grew louder. A blaze of light erupted from the Lava Crown, high above the humans.

"No more talk," Ooloom warned the doctor.

The giant returned his gaze to the humans. His

eyes flared. And like a pack of dying animals, the six companions howled in pain.

"*Prak tara marith yoo,*" said the giant. "The stars. Will fall. And die."

Bryce had never felt such pain. But he held his grip as burning needles stabbed at his brain and his lungs. His skin felt as if it were being pulled from his bones.

Ooloom looked at his army of trolls. "Kill them. Now," he ordered.

The thudding of the troll army surrounded Thora, Pablo, Louise, Zak, and Bryce. The trolls lifted their axes, spears, and clubs over their heads, but the young warriors continued to concentrate.

The doctor's eyes went wide. Time was running out for the young warriors.

Then, suddenly, a rolling shadow ran through the line of troll warriors, sending several trolls flying off the edge of the mesa. It hurtled toward the bodies of the young humans like a storm cloud.

"Uzhk!" screamed Mara.

The friendly troll ran and threw himself at

Ooloom's left foot. He swung his fists into the giant's legs as hard as he could.

*That troll's powerful,* thought Bryce. *But there's no way he could harm that monster.*

But the diversion was enough. The giant's gaze was averted and the pain began to leak away. The young warriors focused again.

Suddenly, a wave of comfort beamed down upon them. It felt like warm sunlight on Bryce's pale skin. He heard a sizzling sound. The golden chains were melting. They dripped harmlessly off their wrists and ankles into puddles of shining liquid at their feet.

"We're free!" cried Bryce.

"Keep holding on to each other!" yelled Thora.

Ooloom growled. "Kill. The traitor!"

The troll warriors aimed at Uzhk from all sides. Instantly, shadows flew overhead as a shower of spears streamed toward Uzhk. The friendly troll cried out as the weapons pierced his hide.

With a mighty shrug of his giant foot, Ooloom threw Uzhk aside. Then, with a colossal roar,

Ooloom's foot rushed downward, crushing Uzhk beneath a ton of living rock. Only a rocky hand and fingers poked out from under the foot. They were motionless.

"Uzhk!" Dr. Hoo yelled. "No!"

# 35

Louise began to steadily glow. A voice rang out from among the humans. "Louise, is that you?" it said.

The girl saw her father, tears streaming down his cheeks. One of his arms hung limply at his side. Louise smiled at him. *Father!* she thought. She closed her eyes and focused as hard as she could.

The doctor dropped to the ground and grasped her hand. He smiled warmly at the others.

"Focus," Dr. Hoo said. "We're nearly out of time."

Dr. Hoo bowed his head and closed his eyes. The others did the same. The band of friends was now complete. All of the companions began to glow with their former radiance.

The doctor raised his hands. The golden chains that held them together broke apart and floated above them. The chains spun swiftly, turning into a blur of light. Then they became one great circle of gold, forming a huge disc. The disc turned on end and started to spin. Slowly at first, and then faster and faster, until a faint whirring sound filled the chamber.

"The band of gold," said the doctor. "Companions of light."

All of them stared at the whirling disc. As it spun faster, it began absorbing the warriors' silver radiance. It began to gleam with a blinding white light.

*Like the sun,* thought Louise. *A band of light!*

The white disc hummed. It moved above Ooloom's crown like a brilliant halo. Suddenly, a tremendous burst of energy erupted across the mesa.

Louise heard a horrible scream as the fiery crown exploded in a torrent of sparks and scarlet light. Cracks began to run along Ooloom's sides. Suddenly, magma spilled from the cracks and onto the ground.

Then the monster violently split into several pieces, each of them tumbling lifelessly to the ground.

The disc, bright as a star, shifted its position to directly above the troll army. The horrid warriors began to stiffen. Then the army came to a sudden stop, petrified.

Zak jumped to his feet. "Yes!" he cried, human again. "We destroyed their ruler!"

The doctor shook his head, grimly. "No," he said. "Not their ruler." He looked at the petrified giant. "He was merely their general. Their ruler, the Great One, lies far beyond this sea of lava."

The waves of lava surrounding the mesa rushed angrily against the cliffs. Dr. Hoo turned to face the young warriors. "Hurry," he said. "We must leave before the Great One comes."

Mara grabbed his shoulder. "Your tower is damaged," she said. "It will not be able to return us to the surface."

"No matter," said Dr. Hoo. He raised his hands. The golden disc slowly changed shape. Now it resembled a golden bowl. "Get everyone inside," he said.

All of the humans — including Zak's parents, Louise's father, and all the others — climbed into the golden vessel.

Once inside, Pablo grabbed Dr. Hoo by the arm. "We thought you betrayed us!" Pablo said. His arm was shaking. The others were listening intently.

Dr. Hoo put his hand on Pablo's shoulder. "I'm sorry, but I had to do it," he said. "Otherwise, the trolls would never have allowed you to get this close to Ooloom. The army would've destroyed you all."

"You still could've told us the plan," Thora said.

"Again, I'm sorry — but I really couldn't," the doctor explained. "The only way they would've allowed you inside this chamber is if you were their prisoners. It had to look real, or they would've killed you on sight."

Dr. Hoo stood. "I know I put you through a lot," he said. "But this was the only way to stop Ooloom. His army was preparing to march. They would've destroyed your homes."

Dr. Hoo turned and glanced around, opening his arms at the family members and friends. "It was also the only way we could save your families. Your loved ones. Yourselves."

Everyone grew silent at the Doctor's words. The Gambles and the Fishers embraced their sons and daughters.

Mr. Tooker brushed Louise's hair from her face. "I can't believe it," he said, smiling down at her. "My little girl is a hero. I'm so proud of you." Louise dug her face into her father's chest, sobbing and smiling.

Dr. Hoo watched the scene. A faint smile crossed his face for a moment, then disappeared. He raised his arms into the air, and the golden bowl began to rise.

# 36

Everyone was silent as the golden bowl began its ascent. In the quiet, the bowl's humming could be heard. It rose high above the mesa floor, up and up into the vast darkness of the great chamber.

Mara took one last look, peering over the edge of the bowl. She gazed down at the dwindling island within the fiery sea, the resting place of her old friend. "Oh, Uzhk," she whispered.

Mara felt a hand on her shoulder. Dr. Hoo was standing behind Mara, tears filling his eyes. He stared down at the boiling lava. Even from this great height they could feel the heat from the molten sea against their faces.

"Uzhk had a powerful heart," Dr. Hoo said. "An almost human one."

Mara stared into the doctor's eyes, seeking answers. "Was his death worth this victory?" she asked.

Dr. Hoo looked upward. "It has to be worth it," he said grimly. "Because this war is far from over."

Darkness closed in on them as the disc continued its ascent toward the surface.

# THE FOURTH NIGHT

Tonight
A star will fade and fall
Tonight
A star will flee the sky
Tonight
A star will burn to ash
Tonight
A star will die.


— from "The Last Battle" by Phoebus Glyver

# 37

The clear, calm waters of the Zion Falls quarry usually reflected the moon and constellations overhead. But this evening, the lake did not reflect the heavenly bodies in the sky. The normally calm water was agitated. An underground disturbance sent slabs of rock tumbling down the quarry's high walls. Giant boulders fell and splashed into the water. The lake trembled and stirred.

Then the lake began spiraling in one direction. A whirlpool formed, with a swirling hole at its center.

Above the lake, lightning flashed in the sky. And from the center of the churning eye of the whirlpool, a golden disc rose into the air.

Shouts and cries came from the surface of the disc. Their voices were loud and happy, their fists pumping in the air in celebration. Dr. Hoo stood above the rest, his three arms hanging from his body.

"The battle has been won," said Dr. Hoo, looking down at his companions. "But the war is not over."

Zak Fisher stood up next to the doctor. "Come on, Doc," he said. "Can't we just celebrate? What happened down there was awesome!"

"Yeah!" said Pablo, sitting by Zak's feet. "We kicked some troll butt down there!"

"It's not over yet," insisted Dr. Hoo. He walked to the center of the golden disc. "True, the gathool have suffered a major defeat. We struck a deadly blow to the heart of their kingdom."

"Yes!" said Zak. "I mean, did you guys see when this disc —"

The doctor held up a hand to silence Zak. "But a wounded enemy is a dangerous one," Dr. Hoo said. "More dangerous than you can imagine. Now, more than ever, we must all stick together."

Thora's gaze caught Pablo's. He looked at her

from across the disc. His eyes glimmered and pulsed like distant stars.

Thora stared up at the stars. *This is where it all began*, she thought, *just three nights ago.*

*Thora . . . Thora . . .*

Thora heard the whisper with her mind, rather than her ears. But she recognized the voice as her brother's.

Bryce lay near Thora on the floor of the golden disc. His hand reached out to hers. "Thora," he said, smiling weakly.

Bryce was slowly returning to normal, but his body was still weak.

"You helped us down there," Thora said, smiling at her brother.

Bryce tilted his head at her. "I did?" he asked.

"Yes," Thora said. "We couldn't have defeated Ooloom without your help."

The monster's name sent a sudden jab of pain through Bryce's body. His grip tightened on Thora's hand. "It's okay," she said. "You're with us. You're safe now."

When Thora closed her eyes, she still saw giant creatures with sharp fangs and claws. And the monster known as Ooloom. His crown of molten lava still burned in her mind.

"Is your brother feeling better?" a voice asked.

Thora turned. Mara was standing behind her. The wind rushed past them both, whipping their long hair into their faces. Thora nodded at the older woman.

Zak's parents were there, too, as were Pablo's parents. Thora's mom and dad smiled back at her. Louise's father was also nearby.

*Thora . . .*

Thora glanced around the area.

*Thora . . . Thora . . .*

*Is that Bryce again?* Thora thought. *It sounds like him. But why is he still speaking with his mind?*

When Bryce had fallen under the trolls' dark influence, they had been able to control him. They had also been able to send his thoughts to other people. Thora thought their power over him had been broken when Ooloom died.

*Zion . . . Falls . . .*

"That's right," Thora said to Bryce. "We're back home."

Bryce shook his head. He looked confused.

Thora noticed that Bryce's eyes gleamed, but not like the light from the stars overhead. And it was nothing like the light she occasionally saw in her companions' eyes.

*Falls* . . . the whisper repeated. *Zion* . . . *falls* . . .

Thora felt an icy coldness grab her heart. *The voice. It isn't Bryce,* she realized.

# 38

Slowly, Dr. Hoo lowered the golden disc onto the lake. The whirlpool had disappeared. The waters of the quarry were calm. As they looked down, they saw the stars glimmering in the water.

The disc settled on the surface like a golden raft. Then it floated gently in the middle of the lake. Dr. Hoo stared at the shore. The light that was reflected in his glasses seemed as red as blood. "Look," he said, pointing.

Above the western edge of the quarry, thick black smoke billowed into the sky. The bellies of the clouds there glowed an angry red.

"Is it a fire?" Thora asked.

"It's the town," said Dr. Hoo. "Zion Falls is under attack."

*Zion . . . falls . . .*

It wasn't only Thora who heard the whisper in her mind. The others heard it now too.

Zak Fisher's father, one of the humans rescued from the trolls, looked up at his son. "I thought you defeated them," he said.

"We outsmarted the general of the troll's army," said the doctor. "But while we were busy underground, they launched an attack up here."

"I should have thought of that," said Mara. "I've read all your books about the *gathool*. I should have known they would trick us."

"They live by deception," said the doctor. "They distracted us from the bigger battle while we were busy fighting Ooloom."

Louise shuddered at the name. "That ugly giant," she said. Her father hugged her tightly.

Pablo stood up next to the doctor. "You said this was a bigger battle?" Pablo asked.

Dr. Hoo returned his gaze to the fiery clouds swarming in the west. "Yes," he said. "Bigger because more is at stake."

Zak shook his head. "I don't get it," he said. "I thought we petrified their entire army."

"That is true," Mara said, nodding. "But as long as their leader lives, they can always add to their army."

"Add?" repeated Pablo. "How?"

"Thora," said Bryce, staring up at her through his broken glasses. "The town . . ."

"Don't worry, Bryce," Thora said. "We'll think of something."

Pablo looked over at the whimpering Bryce. *That's how they replace their fallen warriors,* Pablo thought. The most powerful trolls had minds that could invade human thoughts. An invisible force was reaching out once again to try to take hold of their minds. Pablo felt his memories and thoughts being prodded and poked.

*Stick together,* Pablo told himself. He tried to think about his friends. About the abandoned silo where they had fought together. They were the golden band. The four star-touched companions. Victory was possible, but only if they stayed together.

Thora's face was pinched. Pablo could tell she was trying to fight the dark thoughts too. Zak kept running his shaky fingers through his air. Louise was crying into her father's shoulder.

"Fight it, Bryce," Thora said, holding on to her brother's hand. "Fight it!"

The doctor pointed again toward the western edge of the quarry cliffs. "They are gathering," he said.

Pablo and his companions stared at the cliff edge. The rocks seemed to be moving. *No, not rocks,* Pablo realized. *People.*

Hundreds of townspeople, in fact. Pablo's friends and neighbors who had fled from their burning homes. They stood at the very edge of the quarry, side by side, in a long line. *Like an army,* thought Pablo.

"They're really close to the edge of the cliff," said Thora. "I hope nobody falls."

Just then, the entire line of townspeople bent down. They reached their hands toward the ground.

"What are they doing?" asked Louise.

Pablo's eyes went wide. *They're following orders,* he realized.

Something splashed in the water a few feet away. Louise turned her head to look. "Was that a fish?" she asked.

More and more splashes erupted around the golden disc. Then a loud bang. And another.

"Look out!" Mara shouted.

A fist-sized rock bounced off the metal disc and struck Mara's forehead. She fell to her knees and held her hands to her head. Lionel Tooker shielded Louise with his body. The other passengers huddled together, covering their heads.

A low hum began to fill the air. It grew louder, echoing through the quarry like the roar of a jet engine. Pablo's eyes went wide when he saw what was happening.

The people of Zion Falls were screaming and shouting as they threw rocks and stones.

"Stop it!" Pablo shouted at the townspeople. "We're your friends!"

Dr. Hoo pulled Pablo back from the edge of the disc. "The *gathool* are controlling their minds," he said. "They cannot hear you now."

# 39

Rocks rained down on them like deadly hailstones. Louise was struck on the forehead by a sharp stone.

Mr. Tooker ran to his daughter. "Louise!" he yelled.

A cut opened on Louise's forehead as she sagged into her father's arms.

"We have to get to shore!" cried Pablo.

"Swim for it!" said Zak.

The passengers on the disc leaped over and into the cold waters of the quarry. Everyone began swimming. Lionel Tooker managed to carry his moaning daughter over his shoulder as he paddled. The doctor helped Mara along with one arm while his other two slashed into the water as fast as they could.

At the edge of the quarry, the lake wasn't as deep. Everyone was wading swiftly through the water. When a few of them walked onto shore, the rocks stopped falling.

Pablo stopped where he was in the water and looked up. "They're backing away from the edge," he said.

"Are they leaving?" asked Zak.

A grinding roar burst through the air above them. A pair of lights exploded over the top of the cliff as a huge SUV zoomed off the edge of the quarry, plummeting toward the water.

"What's happening?" shouted Zak.

The SUV plunged into the lake with a violent splash.

"That's Steve Ponto's SUV," said Zak. Pablo saw that Steve and another teenager from their high school were trapped inside the vehicle. Their motionless bodies were pressed against the windshield.

Pablo turned toward Zak. "We have to save them!" he said.

"No," Mr. Tooker said. "They tried to kill us!"

Zak narrowed his eyes. "We can't just let them drown," he said.

Mr. Tooker shook his head and kept moving toward the shore. Most of the disc's passengers were already on land. Thora and the doctor were herding them to safety toward the bottom of the cliff. Only Zak and Pablo remained in the water.

"Zak!" shouted his father from the shore. "Get out of the lake!"

Pablo looked at Zak uncertainly. "He's right," Pablo said. "We need to —"

Suddenly, a loud groan pulled his attention skyward. Another pair of lights was tipping over the edge of this cliff. It seemed to be moving in slow motion. Then they saw that it was no mere SUV. This was a 60-foot-long semi truck.

The axles scraped along the cliff as it teetered over the edge. The truck boomed as it fell sideways against the rocky wall, its huge mass propelling it down toward the doctor and the others.

"Thora, look out!" Pablo yelled.

Thora and Bryce looked up to see the huge vehicle barreling down toward them. She pushed her brother to safety, falling to the ground in the process.

Thora rolled to her back and looked up. The falling semi bearing down on her. She instinctively covered her face with her hands.

A light burst from beside her, pulsing outward like waves in a pool. The light wrapped itself around the semi and suspended it in midair. Then, slowly, it shifted to the side, away from Thora.

Seconds later, the vehicle crashed into the ground with a resounding, bone-shaking crunch.

Thora clambered to her feet. She was about to ask what had happened when she saw Louise hanging over her father's shoulder. The little girl's arms were straight out, light glowing from her fingertips. The light vanished and Louise went limp.

Mr. Tooker gently laid Louise against the cliff wall next to Mara. Their eyes were shut and both of them were breathing raggedly.

Zak and Pablo had been watching from the water as Louise's rings of light swept over them. They both let out a sigh of relief.

"She saved Thora!" Pablo said.

Zak nodded and smiled. "Yep — and now it's our turn," he said. He motioned for Pablo to follow him to the sinking SUV. "Let's go! That thing could sink at any moment."

Pablo pointed toward the shore. "We have to help your parents and the others," he said. "Those people on the cliff are throwing cars at them, Zak! We have to stick together!"

Zak looked toward the shore, then back out to the water. "You go," he said. "I'm not just leaving Steve to die."

"You idiot!" said Pablo. "Do you think you're some kind of hero or something?"

Zak grinned. "Yep," he said. "And you're my sidekick."

Pablo hesitated for only a second. "I'm nobody's sidekick," he said.

Zak just kept grinning. "Well, are you coming?" he asked.

Pablo grunted and started paddling after Zak. Together, they swam frantically toward the SUV.

# 40

The SUV floated in the water. The air trapped inside kept it from sinking too quickly, but the rear window was open a crack and water was starting to seep in. The passengers weren't moving.

"Hurry!" said Zak. He circled to the driver's side of the SUV, while Pablo stayed on the passenger side. They both pulled on the door handles as hard as they could. The doors didn't budge.

Pablo swam behind the car and tried the side door while Zak did the same. Pablo slammed his fist against the window in frustration. "They're all locked," he said.

"Steve, wake up!" Zak yelled through the window.

"Unlock the door!" Pablo cried.

Inside the car, Steve began to stir. Blood was trickling down his face. He tried to sit up, but quickly fell back against the seat and stopped moving.

"They can't help us," said Pablo. "We need something to break the windows."

Zak smashed his fist into the window. He turned and used his elbow, ramming into the window again and again. It didn't even crack the glass

Bubbles gurgled up from under the SUV's hood as the vehicle sank deeper. Zak and Pablo watched helplessly as the inside of the vehicle continued to fill up with water.

The cries from the angry mob traveled across the water, their voices echoing off the quarry walls. "They have us surrounded," Zak said.

The crowd was shouting and chanting together. Pablo recognized what they were saying. *Prak tara. Prak tara.* That's what the creatures had called Pablo and his friends. It meant "children of the stars" in the *gathool* language. Pablo shivered in the cold water. *Why aren't the stars helping us now?* he wondered.

"What are we going to do?" shouted Zak, his eyes darting back and forth between the crowd of people and the sinking car.

The SUV gurgled again and tipped to its side, leaving only a door and part of the body above water. The two boys climbed onto the the side of the SUV. They had to work fast, as it wouldn't be long before the vehicle sank beneath the surface.

Zak screamed in frustration. The scream bounced off the rocky walls surrounding them and grew in intensity. Louder and louder it grew, and deeper. It was no longer the cry of a young man. It was the growl of a ferocious bear.

"Zak!" said Pablo. "Your arm!"

Zak glanced down. His right arm had grown thicker. It was covered in fur. His nails had hardened into thick claws. His muscles bulged and expanded.

With a great roar, Zak crashed his paw into the window. The glass cracked, forming a spider web. Zak brought his bear paw back and threw a second punch, causing the window to shatter.

"Yes!" shouted Pablo. He jumped back into the

water and reached in to unbuckle the seat belt. Quickly, he pulled Steve through the window. Zak grabbed the other boy with his big bear paw and gently pulled him free of the vehicle.

They were just in time. With a final sickening burp, the SUV lurched beneath the water and sank out of sight. Pablo waded away from the wake while holding on to Steve's shirt collar.

Together, Zak and Pablo swam to the nearby golden disc, dragging the unconscious boys behind them. As they reached it, the two boys half pulled, half carried the passengers onto it. Then they climbed aboard and collapsed onto their backs, panting heavily.

"Why did the trolls trap those two inside the SUV?" asked Pablo.

Zak shook his head. "I dunno," he said. He gazed down at his right arm. The fur was slowly disappearing, revealing his normal arm underneath. He flexed his fingers. "Punching that window really hurt."

"It's a good thing your powers kicked in when they did," Pablo said, turning to look behind him. "That SUV's at the bottom of the lake by now."

"Why didn't my whole body change?" asked Zak. "And what about you? No armor, no weapons. A sword would have come in really handy for breaking that glass."

Pablo frowned. "I don't know," he said.

The two boys were silent for a few seconds. They shivered in the night air, their wet clothes clinging to them.

Pablo felt weaker without Thora and Louise by his side. He looked back toward the shore. The crowd was still setting cars on fire and shoving them over the cliff's edge like flaming missiles. When each burning vehicle went airborne, the people cheered. Or screamed. Pablo couldn't tell which. But he did notice that none of the vehicles had people in them.

Pablo's eyes went wide. *Maybe that's why the two passengers were locked inside that SUV,* he thought. *They knew we'd stay out here to help them.*

"We have to get back to the shore!" Pablo said. "They were trying to separate us from the rest of our friends!"

Zak nodded. "You're probably right," he said.

"That would explain why only my arm changed — we were too far away from the others."

Zak lay down at the edge of the disk and started paddling. Just then, a huge bubble began to rise to the water's surface from the same spot where the SUV had disappeared. Another bubble floated up, expanded, and burst. Then another bubble. And another.

Pablo squinted as he looked into the water. A flat, dark object was slowly ascending toward the surface.

"What is that?" whispered Pablo.

"No idea," Zak said.

The dark object floated closer and closer. Soon, Zak recognized it. "It's the roof of the SUV!" he said.

The two watched as the broken window came into view. Then the hood and the door handles peaked above the water.

As the SUV surfaced, the water below the golden disc began to churn and bubble. The bobbing SUV began to rotate. The current caught the disc and dragged it in a large circle around the spinning vehicle.

Pablo froze. He wanted to jump off the disc and

swim toward shore, but he was afraid of what might be lurking underneath the surface.

After all, something had pushed the SUV up from the bottom of the lake. And that same something was still moving it.

Something big. Really big.

# 41

Louise lay unconscious on the ground at the base of the quarry cliff. Thora and Mr. Tooker bent over her. "Louise, can you hear me?" Thora asked.

"We have to get her to a hospital," said Louise's father.

*FWOOM!* Another flaming car crashed into the ground a few yards from where they all sat. Thankfully, they were all huddled beneath the base of the cliff where the rock wall slanted inward at one spot, forming a small shelter.

Thora listened to the howls of the townspeople above their heads. "I don't think we can get her to a hospital," she said.

Thora looked around quickly. Mara lay propped up against the cliff near Thora and the Tookers. Zak's parents were a few feet away along with the others. They were all staring at the fiery destruction raining down near them. She didn't see Dr. Hoo anywhere among them.

Thora turned to Mara. "Where did the doctor go?" Thora asked.

Mara's eyes didn't open. With an effort, she parted her lips. "You must all stick together," she said. Her voice sounded sort of strange, as if she were at the other end of a long tunnel.

"I know," said Thora. "But where is Dr. Hoo?"

Mara didn't respond. She sat motionless with her back against the cliff. She didn't seem to hear the crashes and booms from the falling vehicles.

Mr. Tooker shook his head. "She needs help," he said. "And my Louise needs help."

Thora remembered when she, Louise, Pablo, and Dr. Hoo had joined hands and healed Zak's injured hand. *Maybe we could do the same for Louise now,* she thought.

Thora stooped down and put her hand on Mr. Tooker's shoulder. "Let me take Louise," she said.

Mr. Tooker jerked Louise back. "What are you going to do?" he asked nervously.

"I'm going to find a doctor," said Thora. She wasn't lying. She did want to find Dr. Hoo, as well as Zak and Pablo.

"Then I'm coming with you," said Mr. Tooker.

Thora pointed at Mara. "Someone needs to stay with her," Thora said. "Don't worry. I'll come right back."

"But —" Mr. Tooker began.

Thora looked him in the eyes. "You know your daughter and I have a special connection," she said. "You've seen it." Mr. Tooker nodded reluctantly. "Then please trust me. I'm only trying to help her."

Mara moaned. Mr. Tooker glanced at her. "All right," he said quietly.

"I'll be back as soon as I can," said Thora. She hoisted Louise up into her arms. Then she turned and ran from the cover of the cliff's edge.

Thora sprinted as fast as she could with the extra

burden of Louise's weight. But just by holding the girl, Thora felt stronger and lighter on her feet.

Her path took her through a maze of burning cars and trucks. Her plan was to find the doctor, Pablo, and Zak. She knew that together they could restore Louise to health. At least, she hoped they could.

Thora wanted to put the burning cars between her and Mr. Tooker. She didn't want him to see her moving back toward the shore. He would be too frightened and confused.

Thora scanned the area as she ran, looking for the doctor. *Where is he?* she thought.

Thora kept glancing up from the smashed, fallen vehicles toward the top of the cliff, keeping an eye out for more falling cars.

*Thora . . .*

*Is that Bryce?* Thora wondered. She had completely forgotten about Bryce. He was missing too.

*Thora . . . I'm here . . .*

Thora turned, holding Louise tight.

*FWOOM!* A flaming car crashed behind her, sending a wave of hot air against her back. Thora screamed and ran forward.

"Bryce!" Thora cried. "Where are you!"

Thora saw his head appear over the top of the wrecked car. His face was pale, but covered in soot. His eyes were wild and an eerie smile was frozen on his lips.

Bryce beckoned to her from the broken window. Flames danced along the edges of the car. "Here, Thora," he said. "Hide here!"

"You have to get away from there!" shouted Thora. "It's dangerous."

"They're coming," Bryce said. His voice sounded like a snarling animal. "They're coming to get us."

"Bryce, you have to come with me," Thora said. "We need to find Pablo and Zak and Dr. Hoo."

Bryce saw Louise in Thora's arms. His expression clouded over. "Give me the girl!" he growled.

"What? No!" Thora said, turning Louise away from him. "We have to get her help. We have to find the others!"

Bryce pointed a finger at Louise. "Who cares about her!" he spat out. He jumped down from the car and pressed his hands to his head. He let out a terrible scream. "They're in my head! Just give her to me and they'll let me go!"

Thora shook her head. "Bryce, don't let the *gathool* control you!" she said. "You're stronger than this!"

Bryce ran toward her. He reached out and grabbed Louise's clothes, trying to yank her from Thora's grasp. Thora screamed at him, but Bryce ignored her and kept yanking. His face looked twisted and scared.

Thora pulled at Louise with all her strength. The two siblings each tugged for control of the little girl. But Thora knew that if she pulled any harder, she might harm Louise. So she raised her leg and kicked Bryce square in the chest.

Bryce fell to the grown with a thud. Immediately, sprang back to his feet. "I have to give her to them!" Bryce howled, pointing at Louise. "Then they'll leave me alone!"

"No!" Thora cried.

"She must join the other one," said Bryce. He stepped closer to Thora.

Thora tightened her grip on Louise. Bryce's words made her legs feel weak. Despite the heat of the burning cars around them, an icy chill ran up her neck. "What other one, Bryce?" she asked, taking another step back. "Who are you talking about?"

Bryce grinned. Red light glittered in his eyes. "Who?" he said, cackling like a madman. "Who!"

*Over here . . .* another voice whispered.

Thora glanced around frantically. She knew that voice. As she scurried to the other side of the burning car, she saw him. Thora gasped and almost dropped Louise. Dr. Hoo was lying on the ground next to the car. His face was gripped with pain.

As Thora knelt over him, she saw that Dr. Hoo's third arm was pinned underneath the wrecked car. He was pale. Short, shallow breaths rattled out from his throat.

"Help," he whispered.

# 42

Out in the deepest part of the lake, the SUV's tires were now visible above the surface. It continued to slowly rise from the water like a small submarine.

Zak and Pablo braced themselves, kneeling on the golden disc. The unconscious boys lay next to them.

The SUV was completely out of the water now. Under the SUV's tires was something that looked like a small island. Black rocks and grasses sprouted from its surface.

Zak pointed a shaky finger at the island beneath the SUV. "What is that?!" he cried.

Pablo watched water steam around the island's edges. "Dunno," he said. "But it looks really hot."

*Hroom . . . hroom . . .*

"Oh, no," Zak said, recognizing that deep, hollow booming. It was a sound they had heard in the troll's underground kingdom. The heartbeat of the giant *gathool* general, Ooloom.

"It can't be him," Pablo said. "We turned him and his entire army to stone!"

*Hroom . . . hroom . . .*

Pablo remembered the doctor's words. "Ooloom was merely one of the generals," Dr. Hoo had said. "Their ruler, the Great One, lies beyond."

*The Great One,* Pablo thought. Lord of the *gathool.* He shuddered. It was hard to imagine something worse than Ooloom.

The island rose higher and higher in the middle of the lake. It surged up like a black mountain of clay and stone and fungus. The SUV slid along the slick, wet surface. It slowly rolled down the slope of the rising island until it fell once more into the water, disappearing beneath the surface.

The island reminded Pablo of a monster's head. The rocks and grasses looked like scabs and greasy hair. The island was jet black and had disgusting spots of purplish green. It glistened with thick grease.

Then the island came to a stop. Its center was changing shape. The bumps and knobs began to spread like a fungus.

The knobs stretched in size, absorbing one another. An enormous growth was emerging in the center of the dome-shaped island.

*Hroom . . . hroom . . .*

The pulse throbbed louder. It shuddered through the golden disc and rattled Pablo's bones. He covered his ears with his hands, but it did no good. The sound was all around them. It was inside their heads.

Steve began to moan. His eyelids fluttered. He stared up at Zak. "Fisher?" he said. "What are you doing here?"

"Take it easy, Steve," said Zak. "We're just trying to —"

"What's that noise?" cried Steve. He turned his head. His eyes went wide with fear as he saw the pulsing island.

Pablo could not look away from the fungus-like

mass. It moved as if something living was squirming under the greasy surface.

The thick growth heaved upward. Lumps jutted out from the mass. Other shapes emerged, shapes that resembled arms and legs. The mass became a fully formed creature growing out of the living island. It towered dozens of feet into the air. Four muscular arms thrust from its sides. The nightmarish creature turned its burning red eyes toward the humans.

Steve screamed. Then he passed out.

"Uzhk?" cried Pablo. The thing looked sort of like the creature who had saved them down in the *gathool* kingdom. The troll lifted his mighty arms into the air and roared angrily at Zak and Pablo.

Zak put his arm out to Pablo. "I . . . I don't think that's him," he said.

The monster howled again. His cry was answered by a howl from the surrounding walls of the crater-like quarry.

"And that's not an echo," said Pablo.

Pablo looked toward the rocky cliffs. Their rough sides were thick with long, twisting shadows. But the shadows looked too regular, too evenly spaced. Then Pablo saw the shadows move away from the cliffs.

Not shadows. Tentacles. The arms of a gigantic, squid-like monster. Pablo realized that the dark island in the middle of the lake was merely the top of its head. The underwater beast was huge. Ooloom had seemed like a doll compared to this vast, shapeless monster.

*Thool . . . ooom . . .*

The creature that had sprouted at the top of the misshapen head stared at the boys. Its jaws opened and shut. Raspy sounds sputtered from its tusks. "*Prak tara,*" it bellowed. "How will that meddlesome doctor save you now?"

Zak stood up on the golden disc. "We don't need him," he said. "We'll get rid of your ugly face all by ourselves."

The monster roared. Zak met his roar with one of his own. The boy pumped his arms and screamed into the sky like a wolf howling at the moon.

Pablo stood up and moved right next to his friend. A glow began to spread up Zak and Pablo's feet and legs. It climbed up their chests and traveled across the rest of their bodies.

The silver glow now covered Zak's body. His muscles thickened and his torso expanded. Even though he still looked human, his ferocious growl sounded just like a bear's.

Pablo looked down at his feet. They were fit with shining silver sandals. His hands felt heavy. He clasped them together and saw a single gleaming sword spring into existence from the light in his palms.

Pablo gripped the hilt in his right hand and swung it back and forth in front of him. He grinned and tightened his fingers around its hilt. It felt good to hold the Sword of Orion in his hand once again.

But something was wrong. Pablo touched his chest with his other hand. He wasn't covered with silver armor like last time. He looked over the rest of his body and saw no armor. No helmet. His transformation wasn't complete.

Pablo saw that Zak had grown taller and his muscles looked more powerful, but he had not transformed into the bear of his former battles, either.

This was all the might that the two of them could muster alone. *We need Thora and Louise to complete our transformations,* Pablo realized. He looked at Zak and could immediately tell by the look on his face that Zak knew it too.

"Doesn't matter," said Zak. "We can take this thing on just like we are now."

The troll snickered. It pulled its thick feet off the island's sticky surface. They came away with a ripping sound. It extended its arm toward the sky. A gnarled bone grew out from the limb. The bone solidified into a smooth, sword-like weapon.

From behind him, Pablo heard the giant tentacles thrashing through the waves. It looked like a single blow from one of them could wipe out an entire building. He tightened his grip on his sword. It looked puny and frail next to the monster's weapon. But it was, after all, the Sword of Orion. And it was all he had to defend himself — and his friend.

Zak let out a fierce battle roar. The monster lowered its weapon to its waist and lunged at them with frightening speed.

At the same time, the troll's huge sword arced through the air. Before Pablo could react, its razor-sharp tip sliced into his chest, opening a wide gash in his flesh. Pablo cried out in pain and dropped to his knees. His sword fell from his hands, clanged off the disc, and disappeared into the water.

Pablo's world went dark.

# 43

Thora dropped to her knees next to Dr. Hoo. She ignored the burning cars, the shrieks of the towns-people, and Bryce lingering behind her. All she cared about now was the man lying on the ground before her, wracked with pain, trapped beneath a two-ton flaming wreck.

"Doctor, can you hear me?" she asked.

Dr. Hoo's eyes met hers. "You . . . you must help me," he said quietly, glancing at the limb pinned under the vehicle. "I can't move. My . . . my arm."

Thora trembled. The once-powerful doctor needed her help? She had hoped that he would save her and Louise! Thora looked at the motionless girl in her arms. Thora felt like crying. She felt like giving up.

"Thora, come and hide with me," whined her brother.

"Shut up, Bryce!" Thora snapped.

The doctor reached out to her with one of his free arms. "You must help me," he said again. "I know you can do it."

"I can't," said Thora. She buried her face in Louise's side. "I can't." Her world was falling apart. Her brother was flipping out. Her little friend was dying in her arms. Her other friends were gone and her teacher needed her help.

"I can't do it," Thora said.

The doctor forced a smile through his pain. "The stars can," he said. He gently touched her forehead. "The ones living inside you."

A sequence of images flashed into Thora's mind as fast as she could understand them. She saw *The Book of Stars* from the doctor's library. It opened. Its pages displayed a woman wearing a crown and holding a large jar. The next moment, she saw water and stars spill from the jar's mouth in a shining, silvery flood. Thora remembered the woman was Aquarius, the Water Bearer. The Mover of Floods. The constellation.

Thora remembered how it felt to hold that miraculous jar in her hands. She had poured out water and stars upon her enemies as if they came from her very body.

*But how can I make that jar reappear?* she thought.

"The starlight," said the doctor, as if he were reading her thoughts. "Starlight is in your blood."

The doctor released his grip. He moaned with pain. He grabbed his shoulder, where the car pinned his third arm beneath a ton of glass and steel.

Thora blinked away her tears. Dr. Hoo had saved her in the woods from the first troll she had ever seen. Now it was her turn. She had to help him somehow. She had to think fast.

Thora looked down at Louise. Mr. Tooker had wrapped an old bandana around the girl's forehead to stop the bleeding. But the gash was deep. There was blood on Louise's face.

"How do I do this, Louise?" Thora asked. "Help me. What do I do?"

A gleam of silver caught her eye. Louise's blood was shining on her forehead and cheeks. Thora pulled the girl closer to her chest and closed her eyes. "Help me, Louise," she whispered.

Thora concentrated on the image of Aquarius from the doctor's book. She focused on the crown and the stars and the bottomless jar. Would they help her now? She waited for an answer, but the only sounds she heard were exploding cars and humans screaming.

Thora shivered. She looked down. Cold water was gathering around her ankles and knees in a pool beneath her. When she turned around, she saw that an arm of the lake was creeping up the shore toward her.

Louise's blood glowed brighter. The water surrounding Thora grew deeper. It rose, cover her legs as she knelt next to the doctor. It washed over the doctor's chest and arms, emitting a silver light. With each wave of silver water, the pain on the

doctor's face seemed to wash away. His face calmed, bit by bit, as it lapped against him.

The rushing water was also carving an inlet into the shore. It gathered up the sand and rubble and pulled them toward the lake. Thora felt herself sinking into the damp ground.

She stood up. More water flooded in from beneath her feet. The doctor disappeared beneath its foaming tide. She saw only his wet, flapping coat and one of his hands.

Then the wrecked car groaned. It began to sway. The water had loosened the ground beneath it. Thora felt a burst of energy. She raised her free hand toward the car.

Water and foam blossomed from her fingertips. The car tilted. With a long squeal, the car fell back. It crashed into the water, sending silvery spray into Thora's arms and face.

"Dr. Hoo!" Thora cried. She looked down and reached into the rising foam. She grasped the doctor's hand and pulled it hard. The doctor rose, sputtering, through water and sand. He crawled to his knees, then stood next to her, flexing the arm that had been trapped.

Dr. Hoo smiled at Thora. Then his eyes went wide. "Thora, look out!" he said, pointing behind her.

Thora turned. Bryce was standing in the eddying waves. The reddish gleam in his eyes glowed brighter. In his hand, he held a piece of jagged glass from a broken car window.

"Give me Louise," Bryce demanded. "They're coming! I have to give her to them!"

Dr. Hoo clenched his fists — all three of them. He moved between Bryce and Thora. "You can't trust him, Thora," Dr. Hoo said. "His mind is being manipulated by the *gathool*."

"Give me the girl!" Bryce shouted. He raised the jagged piece of glass and made a menacing slice through the air.

"Don't make me hurt you, Bryce," Dr. Hoo said. "Control yourself — you can do it. Just focus."

Bryce hesitated. His eyes seemed to flicker between red and blue. He shook his head left and right, as if trying to clear his mind. For a moment, he seemed like himself again. "Thora?" he said quietly.

Suddenly, the waves of the lake crashed and boomed behind Bryce. With a long sigh, they reared back and rose into a wall of foam. A shadowy tentacle reached out of the watery wall, wrapped itself around Bryce, and lifted him into the air.

The tentacle twitched, then pulled Bryce under the water and out of sight.

# 44

Pablo coughed and grabbed his chest. Blood covered his hand. He realized he had fallen onto his back on the golden disc.

*Where is the Sword of Orion?* Pablo thought. *And where is Zak?* His vision was hazy, but he could clearly see that only the boys they had pulled from the SUV were with him on the disc now.

Pablo glanced around quickly, blinking his eyes, searching for the Sword of Orion and his friend.

A big spray of water splashed onto the disc behind Pablo. *The tentacles,* he thought. *They're coming for us!*

But it wasn't the tentacles. It was Zak. He was

climbing out of the water onto the dome-shaped island. Onto the head of the monstrous island. That creature.

"What are you doing?" Pablo shouted. Then he froze. In Zak's right hand was the Sword of Orion. Zak had dived into the cold water to retrieve it while Pablo was unconscious.

*My sword looks bigger now,* Pablo thought. He coughed again. The pain stabbed through his chest. More blood seeped onto his shirt. He pressed his hand tightly to the wound, but the blood still gushed out.

Zak looked at the gash on Pablo's chest. Pablo saw the familiar glimmer in his friend's eyes. Zak nodded when his gaze met Pablo's. Zak knew what he had to do without Pablo even saying a word.

Zak roared. He still had not transformed into the bear warrior, but that didn't stop him. With both hands, he raised the huge sword over his head and swung it at the monster. The creature stepped back, narrowly avoiding the deadly blow. The Sword of Orion sank into the sticky surface of the island.

Black fluid seeped out from the gash and a vast bellow trembled up from beneath the water.

*Thooloom* . . .

Dark waters churned and foamed around the edge of the island. The golden disc rocked as the waves lapped against it.

The fungus creature swung its weapon at Zak. He lifted his sword just in time to block the attack. The blades clanged together. The monster attacked a second time, but again Zak deflected the blow. A rain of silver sparks shot outward from the clashing blades.

Then the monster swiftly tossed his sword to another of his four arms.

"Zak! Look out!" cried Pablo.

The young warrior was ready. The troll's blade sliced at Zak from a higher angle, but Zak ducked down as the troll's weapon passed harmlessly over his head.

Back and forth, their blades rang out. The Sword of Orion glowed and flickered, sending silver sparks everywhere. Silver light temporarily lit up the scene each time Zak smashed his sword against the monster's weapon.

Pablo knew that Zak wasn't used to using a sword, but no one would be able to tell by watching him fight. Zak's weapons had always been his bear talons and powerful jaws, but Pablo was amazed at how well Zak fought with a sword. It seemed that Zak's brute, bear-like strength allowed him to swing the weapon with incredible speed. The sword seemed to move on its own, pulling and twisting Zak across the vast head.

Pablo felt guilty. He had dropped the sword into the water. And if he had pushed Zak harder to leave the SUV behind, they would both be on the shore right now next to their companions.

Instead, Zak was out in the middle of the lake battling against a hideous, inhuman creature, and Pablo was slowly bleeding to death.

*This is my fault*, Pablo thought. *We should have all stayed together like Dr. Hoo and Mara told us to.*

The monster made a strange noise. Pablo watched as the tall creature stretched out one of his scaly arms. A second sword grew from its flexing hand.

*There's no way Zak can defend himself now,* Pablo thought. He tried to stand, but his legs gave out and he fell back onto the disc. *He needs my help.*

Pablo knew the four companions always had more strength when they worked together. Together, they had healed Zak's arm after a battle with the fire trolls. Together, they had defeated the Ooloom. Alone, Zak had a fraction of his powers. He wouldn't stand a chance against that monster.

Pablo knew what to do. He took a deep breath and rolled over the side of the disc, plunging into the water.

When his chest hit the cold water, the pain clutched his heart. For a moment, he couldn't move. He began to sink deeper into the inky lake. Far below him, he saw two red fires burning underwater. The two lights blinked at him.

Then Pablo heard the clashing of swords from above the surface. He forced his eyes open wide and clenched his teeth. He couldn't reach out his arms to swim. The injured chest muscles wouldn't let him. Instead, Pablo rolled to his back and flapped his legs.

As he kicked through the water, he swam up toward the edge of the island.

Pablo flapped his legs faster. When he reached the island, he dragged himself up the edge using only one arm. The other hand still gripped his wounded chest.

The fungus-like monster turned toward Pablo. Zak followed its gaze. When he saw Pablo lying next to him, he lowered his sword for a second. "You idiot!" Zak cried. "What are you doing here? You're going to get yourself killed!"

"Your sidekick reporting for duty," Pablo said, struggling to grin through the horrible pain.

Immediately, Pablo could tell that Zak felt stronger. Zak flexed his arms and smiled at his friend.

Then Pablo screamed.

Zak turned back to face the creature. The monster's twin swords were both slashing toward Pablo.

In an amazing burst of speed, Zak dashed toward the monster. With an echoing thud, he slammed his shoulder into the creature's side and sent him reeling backward. The troll almost fell to the ground, but gathered itself at the last moment, managing to stay upright.

The fungus monster bellowed angrily and turned its gaze toward the golden disc. Pablo's eyes went wide as he turned to look. A tall, familiar figure was hovering over the disc, covered in a golden glow. As his boots touched down on the disc, Pablo saw a person cradled in each of Dr. Hoo's arms.

"Thora! Louise!" cried Pablo.

The doctor stared at the fungus monster. "Your time is up," he said. "Accept defeat, or die."

"This is just the beginning!" the creature bellowed. "It is you who must accept death! It is you who must die!"

Then the monster roared. It lifted its arm and threw a sword at the disc with incredible speed. It flipped end over end as it flashed toward the doctor.

The doctor shifted his weight and dropped

Thora and Louise onto the disc. A split second later, the monster's sword sliced off Dr. Hoo's third arm at the elbow. He collapsed on the disc as his severed arm splashed into the water. Thora screamed.

Zak's eyes went wide as the beast raised the other sword over Dr. Hoo's fallen body, preparing to finish the job.

"No!" shouted Zak. He swung the Sword of Orion at the beast and knocked the sword from its hand. The monster's eyes shifted to Zak. The troll immediately lunged sideways at him. Its massive jaws opened wider than Pablo thought possible.

With a sickening crunch, the monster's jaws clamped onto Zak's torso and lifted him off his feet.

Zak and Pablo both cried out at the same time. The monster lifted Zak high overhead, shaking his bleeding body like a rabid dog.

"Zak!" shouted Pablo.

"No!" Thora cried.

A horrible sound came from the monster's jaws as Zak's bones snapped, but he somehow managed

to hold on to the Sword of Orion. With his remaining strength, Zak plunged the blade into the monster's head — all the way up to the hilt.

Zak released the sword and went limp. The troll dropped him, and he fell in a heap onto the island. The monster stumbled, retching and coughing. It tried to pull out the sword, but it couldn't reach.

The island heaved and jerked underneath. Pablo saw that the monster was attached to the island by a long cord. As the troll thrashed and writhed, its pain was shared by that creature below the water.

Finally, the monster began to crack and crumble. Three arms fell to pieces like shattered pottery. In seconds, the creature had crumbled into a mass of dirt and clay. In the middle of the pile laid the Sword of Orion, glinting in the moonlight.

The island thrashed wildly. *A wounded enemy is a dangerous one,* Pablo remembered. He crawled over to the fallen sword. He grabbed it and raised the Sword of Orion over his head. With every ounce of strength he had left, he brought the sword down, plunging it into the center of the island.

A hideous shriek rose up from beneath the water. The island shuddered. Its long tentacles curled up and surged toward Pablo. Thora and Louise suddenly appeared at Pablo's side. Kneeling, they placed their hands on top of Pablo's.

A ball of shimmering light grew around their hands. Lights twinkled in the water around them. The stars overhead were motionless, but their reflections on the waves quivered and stirred.

The island shook violently. "Hold on!" yelled Thora.

The star reflections whirled around them like a blizzard of fireflies. The light from the sword grew more intense as the lights danced around it.

*Like moths to a flame*, Pablo thought.

Suddenly, the starry lights all flew toward the center of the island. The stars rushed toward the sword and passed through the companions' hands. Light dived down the length of the blade and into the creature below. The sword hilt blazed like the sun.

Thora reached out and grasped Zak's limp hand.

The light grew brighter, and an explosion rocked the quarry. The surprised cries of the townspeople carried across the lake.

Slowly, the starry light faded. Small cracks ran along the island's surface. When Pablo reached his hand down to touch the island, he felt that it had turned to lifeless stone.

"Did we do it?" whispered Thora. Pablo looked over the edge of the island. The burning eyes from below had vanished.

Dr. Hoo looked at Thora and nodded. He looked relieved, despite his missing arm. "Thooloom was the father — the creator — of the *gathool* species," he said, a faint smile on his lips. "They are born from his body, created in his image. With him dead, and their army destroyed, the war is over."

Pablo felt the cold, hard stone beneath his hands. He traced a finger along the jagged cracks that ran along the petrified troll's head. "So, he's dead?" Pablo asked. "For good?"

Dr. Hoo nodded. "For good," he said. "The world is safe now. Because of you."

Thora sank to the ground, relieved. Pablo smiled.

But his smile faded when he heard Louise crying. She was leaning over Zak, tears streaming down her face.

Pablo crawled across the sticky clay toward them. He shook Zak's shoulder. "Zak, wake up," he said. "It's over now."

Zak didn't move. Blood streamed from a dozen wounds in the boy's torso and arms. Then his eyes fluttered, opening halfway.

"Zak!" yelled Pablo.

Zak smiled weakly. "Pablo?" he asked in a raspy voice. His eyes gleamed with strange unearthly light that Pablo had seen many times before. But now it was much more faint.

Pablo grinned. "Yeah, it's your sidekick," he said. "I'm right here."

Thora and Louise bent down next to Pablo. Behind them, Dr. Hoo stood silently.

"We're all here," said Thora.

"We'll take you home," said Louise.

Zak coughed. His body trembled. The starlight

flickered in his eyes. "You're the best friends . . . anyone could ever have." he said.

Zak blinked his eyes once, twice, then closed them for the last time.

# 45

Pablo felt a hand turn his body over. A dark shadow loomed over him. He heard the splash of water nearby.

"You passed out," said Thora. "We brought everyone here."

Pablo rolled onto his side. He was lying on the far eastern shore of the quarry lake. Red clouds from the smoking town hung above the western cliffs. A mass of burning cars littered the opposite shore.

"Zak!" Pablo cried, remembering what had happened. "Where's Zak?"

"Careful," Thora said. "You've been through a lot."

Pablo clutched at his chest. It still ached a little, but the wound was gone. He saw Louise sitting next to Thora. A few feet away, the doctor was kneeling over Zak's motionless body.

"Is . . . is he okay?" asked Pablo.

Thora's eyes were filled with tears. "We were able to heal your wound," she said. "And Louise's head."

"The doctor lost an arm," Louise said sadly.

Dr. Hoo smiled down at her. "I'll be fine," he said.

Pablo sat up a little higher. "Is Zak all right?" he asked, his voice trembling.

Dr. Hoo didn't respond. He kneeled over Zak. Pablo couldn't tell, but it looked like the doctor was crying.

Thora shook her head sadly. "We tried," she said to Pablo. "We tried really, really hard."

Pablo hung his head. For a few moments, no one spoke.

Louise tugged at Thora's arm. "Tell him about Mara," she said.

"Is Mara . . . dead?" asked Pablo.

Thora shook her head. "She's not dead," she said. "Mara left Zion Falls. The doctor said she finished what she came to do."

"Well, where is she now?" Pablo asked.

Louise pointed to the sky above the quarry. "She's up there," she said. "With her sisters. The stars."

Thora turned toward Dr. Hoo. "Then Mara used to be one of us?" asked Thora. "Like it says in *The Book of Stars*?"

The doctor turned around slowly. His face was pale and gaunt. "Yes, Thora," he said quietly. "Like in *The Book of Stars*. And tonight, the book will have a new page."

Pablo gazed at his fallen friend. His lips trembled.

Dr. Hoo placed a hand on Pablo's shoulder. "He was a true warrior," Dr. Hoo said. "The mighty Arcturus. The Great Bear."

"But we're all together now!" Pablo said. "We can join hands — join our powers, like we did before. We can bring Zak back!" He looked left and right at his friends, then at Dr. Hoo. "Can't we?!"

Dr. Hoo frowned. "There are some things even the stars can't do," he said.

"No!" shouted Pablo. "But Zak . . ." A sob burst up from his throat.

"Zak sacrificed himself for his friends," said the doctor. "That is the last — and greatest act — a warrior can do."

"I would rather have died for him," Pablo whispered.

"Me too," said Louise. Thora nodded. Tears streamed from her eyes.

Dr. Hoo smiled faintly. "And that's why the four of you were chosen by the stars," he said.

Pablo walked over to Zak's body. He knelt down next to Dr. Hoo. Thora and Louise knelt next to him. Pablo couldn't speak.

Louise reached out a hand and placed it gently upon Zak's chest. "Brave, big bear," said Louise. "We'll never forget you."

Thora nodded. "Never, Louise," she said.

Dr. Hoo put his arms around their shoulders. "Zak's time on Earth is finished," he said. "But he will never be forgotten. It's time for him to take his place among the stars."

Dr. Hoo placed his left hand on Zak's chest. He closed his eyes and concentrated. The friends watched in awe as a silver light slowly began to glow beneath the doctor's palm.

The light seemed to come from deep within Zak's body. Its tendrils wrapped around the doctor's hand, swirling in his palm like a dancing light.

The doctor stood and raised his arm. The light rocketed from his hand and shot into the sky.

"Farewell, Arcturus," said the doctor.

Pablo took the hands of Thora and Louise. All of them watched as a single star blinked into existence above Zion Falls, joining its ancient companions in the heavens.

# EPILOGUE

## *SEVERAL WEEKS LATER . . .*

Snow dusted County Road One where a rusty school bus squealed to a stop. Two girls climbed off together. It was not their regular stop. Bundled up tightly in coats, scarves and gloves, they made their way up a rough dirt driveway. The tree branches overhead were bare. The wind was bitterly cold.

At the end of the long driveway stood a huge stone house. At the top of a stone tower, dark windows, like empty eyes, stared across the winter fields.

"Dr. Hoo," called out Louise as she and Thora stepped inside.

They called again. There was no answer.

Step by step, they climbed to the doctor's library

at the top of the tower. The room was still charred from the battle with the fire trolls. Books and shelves lay scattered across the blackened floor.

Thora was quiet. After the last month, after the terrible battles, after losing her brother and her friend in one nightmarish night, she couldn't bear it if the doctor was gone, too. "Where did he go?" asked Louise.

Something crackled behind them. The girls turned and stared at a book lying on the floor. "*The Book of Stars!*" shouted Louise.

The large volume lay open. Its pages shuffled back and forth, as if moved by invisible hands. The two girls edged closer, carefully watching its moving pages.

"Why is it doing that?" asked Louise.

Thora stared at the colorful pages. Stars and constellations whirled past. Names and shapes she had never seen before. "I think," she said with a smile, "that the book is looking for more heroes."

# DR. HOO'S GUIDE TO THE GATHOOL LANGUAGE

The gathool language doesn't have many words, and the pronunciation is usually straightforward. However, many gathool words have several meanings, so translating the language is quite a challenge. Here are some of the words I've managed to decipher.

AGNA GATHOOL — the descendents of true dragons, the agna gathool, or fire trolls, resemble dinosaurs. They have red-hot tongues, and are capable of spraying fire from their jaws.

BAZHARGAK (buh-SHAR-gok) — palace of night. A bazhargak, or dark tower, is a gathool method of transportation.

DRAKHOOL (druh-KOOL) — trolls of the earth. The gathool see the drakhool as their soft-hearted, inferior siblings.

CROATOAN (croh-uh-TOH-uhn) — moving bridge. Croatoans are used to move large numbers of trolls between locations. A bazhargak is a type of croatoan used by warriors.

GATHOOL (guh-THOOL) — true trolls. The gathool use the word to describe all of troll-kind, but reserve another word for drakhool, their peaceful brethren.

HOOLOO (hoo-LOO) — one with two souls. A PERSON who is born from one troll parent and one human parent. Also called a half-blood.

HROOM (har-OOM)—there is no standard definition for this word. It sounds like a drum, and serves as a rally cry for troll leaders.

OOLOOM (oo-LOOM)—harvester of souls. Ooloom is an honorary title given to the leader of the troll army. Only Thooloom, also known as The Great One, commands more power and respect.

PRAK TARA (PROK TAR-uh)—the bearers of light. The phrase refers to the children of the stars, or the star-touched ones, who are fated to oppose the trolls in a grand battle for control of Earth.

THOOLOOM (thoo-LOOM)—the Great One. They say he has surfaced only once before — thousands of years ago — causing a cataclysmic effect that wiped out nearly all life on the surface. If unopposed, his presence means just one thing: the skies will be filled with darkness, snuffing out the light from the stars above for centuries to come.

THYUL HU (THEE-uhl HOO)—ones who cannot be trusted. The phrase can refer to snakes, servants, or treacherous individuals.

UZHK (OOSHK)—tranquil one. Uzhk is a drakhool, and a friend of mine. He is one of the few trolls who seems to like humans.

# NOTES ON BAZHARGHAKS

The gathool use their bazharghaks, or dark towers, for three reasons. First, they are fast, direct, and provide shelter from the sun's harmful rays.

Secondly, the drilling motion of the towers loosens the ground, making the earth unstable, giving the nimble trolls an advantage on uneven terrain.

Thirdly, the towers allow the gathool to create a direct path to the surface so that reinforcements can travel through the tunnel if backup is needed.

In order to have any chance at surviving a troll invasion, the bazharghaks must be stopped from reaching the surface.

# THE GATHOOL HIERARCHY

Above all else, trolls respect power. To become an Ooloom, or leader of the gathool army, a troll must prove he is stronger than all the rest. That is no easy task, considering that every troll is expected to do battle from the point they're able to lift a spear until the day they die.

The crowning of an Ooloom is a fearsome event. All challengers for leadership of the troll army present themselves as candidates. They choose their weapons, and the group melee begins. At the end of the chaotic battle, the last gathool standing has the Lava Crown placed atop his head, identifying him as the Ooloom. The title lasts until death, whether from old age, or at the hands of a troll looking to take his place.

Only Thooloom — or the Great One — has more power over the gathool than an Ooloom. However, no one has seen the Thooloom and lived to tell the tale.

## NOTES ON THE PRAK TARA

The powers given to the prak tara, or the children of the stars, come from constellations. I can confirm that this is true, as I have seen the stars choose human warriors first-hand.

The scope of the prak tara's powers is limited only by their imaginations. The celestial powers bring out the strongest parts of each individual. Additionally, the closer the prak tara are to each other, the stronger they become. Seeing Zak, Louise, Thora, and Pablo combine their might was the most awe-inspiring thing I've ever seen.

I do not know how the stars decide which four humans to choose. But from my experiences with this generation's prak tara, there is no question that the constellations pick wisely. It has been my life's honor to help Thora, Pablo, Louise, and Zak unite together with their powers. If it weren't for them, I would be dead . . . and so would you.

*Benjamin K. Hoo*

# ABOUT THE AUTHOR

As a boy, MICHAEL DAHL persuaded his friends to celebrate the
Norse gods associated with the days of the week. (Thursday was
Thor's Day, his favorite!) Dahl has written the popular Library of
Doom series, the Dragonblood books, and the Finnegan Zwake
series. As a Norwegian lad from the Midwest, he believes in trolls.

# ABOUT THE ILLUSTRATOR

BEN KOVAR was born in London. He trained in film and animation and spent several years as an animator and art director before moving into writing and illustrating fiction. He lives in an attic, likes moisture, and has a fear of sunlight and small children.